Spiked!

Other titles by Sandra Glover

Spiked!
sandra glover

WOODMILL HIGH SCHOOL

Andersen Press • London

First published in 2005 by
Andersen Press Limited,
20 Vauxhall Bridge Road, London SW1V 2SA
www.andersenpress.co.uk

The right of Sandra Glover to be identified as the author of this
work has been asserted by her in accordance with the Copyright,
Designs and Patents Act, 1988.

British Library Cataloguing in Publication Data available
ISBN 1 84270 431 1

Jacket design by Sara Freeman

Typeset by FiSH Books, London WC1
Printed and bound in Great Britain by Mackays of Chatham Ltd.,
Chatham, Kent

Chapter 1

Debra snatched the piece of paper, pushing her way out into the courtyard, ignoring the shrieks and screams. Her hands were shaking, her eyes blurred as she looked down the page, trying to take it all in.

'Well?' Beth was asking.

'I got an A in French!' said Debra, totally stunned. 'I don't believe it! French!'

'Why don't you shout a bit louder, Debs?' a voice sneered. 'So we can all hear about your A grades.'

Debra turned to see Amy Parker walking past with her mate, Ellie.

'Sorry,' Debra muttered. 'Er, how did you get on?'

'I did OK,' said Amy. 'Not as well as you, obviously, but then I'm not a swot, am I? Some of us like to have lives, don't we, Ellie?'

'Take no notice,' said Beth, grabbing Debra's results from her, as Amy walked on. 'Hey, you got an A in history as well...Brill! That'll shut Mr Mason up! Lit A*...'

Debra didn't hear the rest because Tonya and Safira arrived, leaping at her, hugging her, almost squeezing her breath away. Not that Debra needed to hear. She'd already memorized them. And they were good. Very good. Much better than she'd expected. Good enough to make months of tedious revision and the total suspension of her social life seem worthwhile ... no matter what Amy Parker said.

'What about you?' she managed to ask as she untangled herself.

The girls passed their results sheets round.

'Bloody hell, Beth!' Safira yelled. 'I thought me and Tonya had done well till I saw that. A★s! They're all A★s!'

But she said it without malice. No one was surprised that Beth had outclassed them. She always had. Right from infants. Bit of a natural was Beth.

Papers were still being passed back and forth, results analysed, congratulations and, in some cases, commiserations exchanged when a car swung into the car park, its door slamming as someone staggered out.

'Hey, Debs,' the man shouted. 'Over here. Bring your friends over.'

'It's Tim,' Debra said. 'Tim Simmonds. Photographer. From Mum's paper.'

'Is he OK?' said Beth. 'He looks a bit ...'

Drunk.

Beth didn't actually say it. She didn't have to. It was obvious enough from the unshaven face and crumpled clothes he'd probably slept in. Let alone the stink of whisky as they got closer.

'Should he be driving?' Safira whispered. 'I mean, how does he do his job? If he's an alco?'

'He isn't,' Debra hissed, not wanting to give too much away, not even to her best friends. 'He's just drinking a bit heavily, that's all. It's a recent thing.'

'Debs, my lovely!' Tim shouted, before anyone could ask more questions. 'How did it go?'

'Great,' said Debs, showing him her results. 'I did fine!'

'More than fine!' said Tim, grinning at her. 'I'll just check with your teachers if it's OK to do the photo. Can't be too careful, these days! Don't go away!'

Minutes later he was back.

'Right, come on, girls. How about a picture by the gate? That's it. Move in closer. Come on, smile! You're supposed to be happy. Wave those . . . results around.'

'I'm happy,' said Omar Choudhray bouncing over. 'I passed everything. How about a picture of me?'

'Sorry,' said Tim. 'I'm after a bit of glamour here. Our readers want brains *and* beauty.'

'I can do beauty,' said Omar, rolling his tee shirt up to his midriff and striking an exaggerated girly pose.

'Very nice,' said Tim, smiling. 'But you can't compete with our lovely Debra.'

'Girls!' said Omar, reluctantly standing back. 'It's always girls, innit? No wonder lads don't bother trying. No one's interested in what we do.'

'Oh come on then,' said Tim. 'Perhaps we could do Beauty and the Beast. Stand at the back. And Debs, you come forward a bit. That's it. Wait a minute, I think we could do with a couple more. How about you, love?'

He'd turned to Miriam, who was standing a little way off. Tall. Blonde hair. Enormous green eyes. Generally accepted to be the most stunning girl in the school. Even now, with the dark rings under her eyes and her natural

3

slimness beginning to look dangerously skinny, Miriam was still gorgeous.

'Don't you think one member of my family plastered over your bloody paper is enough?' she snapped.

'Oh well,' Tim said, looking bemused as Miriam walked away. 'You can't win 'em all. How about the lad with the ginger hair? No, not there, you're too tall! At the back. Oh and the girl in the red, strappy top. Come on, in there next to Debs. That's it. Hold it. One more. Great!'

There was no sign of Tim slurring his words or of his hands shaking. No hint that the pictures, which would appear in that night's paper, would be anything less than perfect. Somehow he was still managing to do his work, even if there had been a dozen complaints recently about his breath, his lateness, his scruffiness.

He made notes of their names and grades and gave Debra a quick hug as he left.

'Congratulations, love,' he said. 'You'll be off celebrating tonight, will you?'

'Family meal,' said Debra, pulling a face. 'The big party's Saturday night.'

She waved to Tim as he got into his car but her attention was already elsewhere. She'd turned towards the main entrance, wondering where Miriam had got to. Tonya had said Miriam was disappointed with her results. Though they weren't that bad, under the circumstances, Tonya had stressed.

Debra couldn't see Miriam but dozens more pupils and several teachers had come out. Debra's dad wasn't amongst them. Probably still busy. Checking statistics. Dealing with problems. As Deputy Head, he'd have been one of the first to see the results. But he hadn't phoned her. Or offered any sneak previews. She'd had to come in like everyone else.

As she drifted towards the door Marc Cavendish burst out, shouting and swearing at no one in particular. Debra's hands automatically went up to tidy her hair. Her eyes ran a quick check over her skirt and her mouth fixed itself in what she hoped was a dazzling smile. Only her legs let her down, going so weak she had to stop walking.

'Get a grip, Debs,' said Beth. 'Think cool.'

Cool! How could she possibly stay cool around Marc Cavendish? He was just so completely and utterly gorgeous. Not that it mattered, Debra thought. He hadn't even noticed her. He'd found a different audience. His usual clique of football mates – Omar, Benny and half a dozen others.

'He says I've got to re-sit maths, the stupid...'

No one, thought Debra, as Marc yelled a string of expletives, could use quite so many swear words in the same sentence as Marc in one of his moods.

'And English lit!' he said. 'I mean what's maths and bloody English got to do with A-level PE? I got 5 A–C grades. I got enough, didn't I? Bs in PE and IT! And what does he do? Gives me a flaming lecture about how I've got to stop pissing about and get down to some proper work. He's always picking on me. Just like he picked on our Dean!'

By the way Marc had turned and scowled at her, Debra had an idea of who 'he' might be, even though she was fairly sure her dad wouldn't have used the phrase 'pissing about'.

'He's a right psycho, he is,' said Marc, kicking an empty Coke can at Benny. 'Told me if I didn't stop mouthing off, I wouldn't be back for sixth form at all.'

Debra took a deep breath waiting for the inevitable punch line. Her dad knew Marc almost as well as she did. Marc, at best, was a good laugh, famous for being able to charm his way out of most things, if and when he wanted to. But once he got started on one of his wobblers, there was no stopping him.

'Well I told him, didn't I?' Marc was confirming. 'Exactly where he could stick his sixth form. Stuff him. Stuff the school. I wouldn't come back here if they bloody paid me.'

He bent down, picked up a stone and swung round to face the office window.

'Marc, don't!' Debra screamed, lurching forward.

But it was OK. Omar had already grabbed him. Benny had wrenched the stone from his grip and was steering him away towards the gates. The girls could still hear Marc shouting and swearing when he was half way down the road.

'He didn't mean it,' said Debra, trying to convince herself. 'You know what he's like when he gets going. He doesn't really want to leave. All his mates are coming back. And Mr Mason won't let him leave, will he? He needs Marc for the teams.'

'By the sound of things,' said Tonya, 'your dad won't have him back anyway.'

'Oh, Mr Mason'll talk Dad round,' Debra said.

She paused. Come to think of it, Allan Mason was the last person Dad would listen to. Although Dad never spoke much about other staff when Debra was around, it was obvious he didn't like Allan Mason. It wasn't his teaching that was the problem. Mr Mason taught history well and PE brilliantly. And Dad was grateful for all the extra work Mr Mason put in with the teams. But Dad also thought Allan was arrogant. A bit too friendly with some of the kids. Wasn't keen on the fact that he'd dated a couple of ex-pupils.

There'd been a big stink last year when Zara Fisher's parents had complained to the governors. Mr Mason had been close to losing his job. In fact, if it had been Dad's decision, he might well have lost it. But the governors saw it differently. Zara had already left school. The relationship was over anyway. And Zara had lied about being pregnant. So it was all covered up. Apart from the fact that every single person in school knew about it, of course.

'Maybe,' Debra decided, on reflection, 'I should talk to Dad myself.'

'And you think Marc would thank you for it, yeah?' said Beth. 'You think he'll be so gushingly grateful that he'll ask you out again?'

'I'm not talking about going out with him again,' said Debra.

'Good,' said Tonya. ''Cos last time he treated you like shit.'

7

'He didn't,' said Debra, as Beth and Tonya exchanged glances. 'He just wasn't ready for a heavy relationship, that's all.'

'He's pathetic and immature, Debs,' said Beth, quietly. 'You just can't see it, that's all.'

Immature? How could Beth say that? Marc looked so much older than the other Year 11 lads, for a start, and he could be dead romantic when you got him on his own. Her friends never really saw Marc at his absolute best and she was about to tell them just that when Miriam came out.

'Where'd you get to?' Beth asked.

'I went to see Mr Cardew,' she said, looking at Debra.

'Why?' Debra asked. 'Why did you need to see Dad? Tonya said you got the grades you really needed. You don't need to change any of your A-levels or anything, do you?'

'No,' said Miriam. 'But I won't be doing them here.'

'What do you mean?' said Beth.

'We're moving,' said Miriam.

No one asked why. They all knew.

'Mum reckons we should stick it out,' Miriam said. 'But Dad's had enough. There was another letter yesterday.'

Tears were starting to form as she spoke. Beth and Tonya steered Miriam to a bench, positioning themselves either side of her. Debra hung back, feeling somehow guilty. As though it was her fault that Mum's paper had covered the case. Brought Miriam's family to the attention of the people who were now sending hate mail.

8

'It's not just Dad,' said Miriam. 'It's me. I can't stand it. I can't stand the looks, the whispers. I'm not getting any sleep.'

'Nobody's whispering,' said Beth.

'So it's all in my mind, right?' Miriam snapped. 'Well you should read some of the letters. I don't know how they got on to us. How they got our address. It's not as though we've even got the same surname as Uncle Gordon. But they're maniacs, these people. They don't let go. They're not ever going to let go. But it's not just them.'

'What do you mean?' Beth asked.

'Not just the nutters and their hate mail,' said Miriam. 'It's ordinary people too. Friends, neighbours, people we've known for years. They treat us differently now. Half of them avoid us altogether and the other half are full of false sympathy and morbid curiosity. Wanting to know all the gory details.'

'So where are you moving to?' Tonya asked. 'When are you going?'

'Well, the house is sold.'

'Sold!' screamed Tonya. 'I didn't even know you'd put it up for sale.'

Miriam shrugged.

'So hopefully next week,' she said. 'If everything goes to plan. Definitely by the end of the summer. But I can't tell you where. Dad says we're not to tell anybody.'

'I'll miss you!' said Beth, throwing her arms round Miriam.

Debra stood, clutching her results, scrunching the

9

paper into a tight ball, as any euphoria she had left slowly drained away.

Nothing was working out like it was supposed to. Marc wouldn't be back next year. And now Miriam. Driven away, driven half mad, by a scandal that had nothing to do with her. Not really. Why should Miriam have to suffer because of what her uncle had done? No matter how sick it was. And she was certainly suffering. She looked permanently ill, she'd taken loads of time off school, lost all her sparkle, all her confidence. Not to mention watching her parents' marriage disintegrating under the pressure. Wasn't all that bad enough without people making it worse?

'What about Saturday night?' Tonya was asking. 'You'll still come to the party, won't you?'

'I don't think so,' said Miriam.

'You've got to,' said Beth.

Bright, bubbly Beth who held them all together.

'It'll be our last big night out together,' she insisted. 'So if you don't turn up at Tonya's by seven, I'm coming round to your house to kidnap you, OK?'

'I'll see,' said Miriam, as a car horn sounded on the drive. 'Gotta go. Mum's here.'

'Do you think she'll come?' said Tonya. 'To the party?'

Debra nodded, knowing that Beth would be on the phone to Miriam later, persuading, cajoling. Miriam would probably come. But would Marc? A party wouldn't be a party at all, without Marc to liven things up.

'Well done, girls,' said a voice.

Dad's 'teacher' voice. Debra looked up. Her dad was always careful about being professional, distanced, when there were other people around. But he couldn't help himself this time.

'Brilliant, Debs!' he said, despite the fact that both Beth and Tonya's results had been even better. 'Well done, love.'

'Yeah, well done *all* of you,' said Mr Mason, who'd followed him out. 'All right, Bob? Got all your statistics sorted out?'

Debra saw her dad wince. His name was Robert. He'd tolerate Rob from people who knew him really well but Bob, he hated. And Debra could tell from Allan Mason's smirk that he knew it.

'Can I have a word, Bob?' Mr Mason said. 'About Marc Cavendish.'

Mr Cardew nodded, wearily, and turned to go inside. He paused, looked back at Debra.

'So what did your mum say then?' he asked.

Debra's hand went up to her mouth.

'I haven't phoned her yet!' she said. 'Or Lori. I can't believe it. I completely forgot! I'll phone them both now.'

Fiona Cardew paused before picking up the phone. She looked at the woman who'd burst into her office fifteen minutes earlier and was now pacing up and down in tears.

'I'm sorry,' Fiona told her. 'I won't be a minute. Hi, Debra. How did it go? Five As ... and five A*s! Debs, that's fantastic!'

11

'Mum,' said Debra. 'Is everything all right? I can hear someone crying.'

'Yes,' said Mrs Cardew, glancing at the woman. 'I'm fine. But it's a bit awkward. Look, can I phone you back?'

Fiona put the phone down, feeling vaguely guilty but knowing that Debra would understand. She turned her attention to the woman. She was a large lady. Not fat but heavily built. Huge feet and hands. Her face was strongly defined, almost masculine. She wasn't, Fiona guessed, the type to cry easily.

'Mrs Hall,' Fiona said, offering a tissue from the box on her desk. 'Please. Sit down.'

The woman sat, dabbing her eyes with the tissue, trying to compose herself.

'I'm sorry,' she said. 'I don't know why I've come. It won't do any good, will it? You'll put it in the paper whatever I say, won't you?'

Fiona nodded.

'I have to,' she said calmly. 'It's not something I can choose to ignore. It's a big case.'

Big! Who was she kidding? It was massive. One of the biggest and most sensitive stories the paper had dealt with since Fiona had been promoted to editor four years ago. Last year three men had been arrested as part of a national swoop on the downloading of child porn on the net.

Three arrests in a town like theirs was news enough. Add to that the fact that two of those men were well-known figures in the community: Councillor Gordon Wilcox, sentenced two months ago, now serving five years and Dr James Hall whose trial was due to start next month. In between was the story currently running in the paper. Probably the worst of the bunch. If you could quantify things like that. A man who'd been accessing pictures of kids as young as two. Toddlers. Babies really. Girls and boys alike.

To his friends and family he'd seemed like a normal, regular bloke. A 33-year-old plumber. He was married, for heaven's sake, with two young kids of his own.

Fiona shuddered. It was unthinkable. Completely unthinkable.

'My husband's innocent,' Mrs Hall said, starting to cry again. 'He's not like the others. It was a mistake. It was all a mistake. He was doing research into child abuse. For an article he was writing. It led him to look at child prostitution. He accessed some of the sites, thinking they were factual! Not knowing how bad they were.'

She paused, for a moment, perhaps sensing Fiona's cynicism.

'He was shocked by what he found. The extent of it. How easy it was to get hold of. And he decided to focus his article on sex abuse. Well, he had to look at the sites, didn't he?' she added. 'How else was he supposed to do the research? That's all he was doing. Research. And they're treating him like a dangerous criminal. They won't even let him out on bail!'

She stood up. Put her palms flat on the desk and stared at Fiona.

'My husband's not a paedophile, Mrs Cardew,' she said.

13

'He's a good man. He's 52. He's never been in any sort of trouble. Not even a flaming parking ticket! We've been married nearly thirty years. Do you think I don't know him after all that time?'

Fiona hesitated, wondering whether Mrs Hall was expecting an answer. Or what answer she could possibly give. We all think we know people, Fiona reflected. She'd been pretty certain she'd known Gordon Wilcox. They'd worked together a lot over the years. Attended the same parties, the same functions. Not to mention the fact that he was Miriam's uncle. Miriam, one of Debra's close circle of friends who'd been together since infant school.

People had respected Gordon as a man, as a local politician and as a devoted parent who'd brought up his son alone since his wife walked out twenty years ago. He was, to use an old-fashioned term, a gentleman.

But one who'd apparently been leading a double life. Unlike Dr Hall, Gordon had pleaded guilty. Said he'd been drawn to internet porn out of curiosity at first. One thing had led to another. First adults. Women. Then girls. Younger girls. It had all been so easy. So seductive. So addictive, he'd claimed. Was that what had happened to this woman's husband? Or was it a genuine mistake?

'Are you listening?' Mrs Hall suddenly shouted. 'Are you listening to what I'm telling you? My husband's innocent and you're going to make him out to be some dirty little pervert! Just like you did with Gordon Wilcox. Just like you're doing with this plumber. Destroying lives!'

Fiona sighed. They'd tried to avoid sensationalism in

the paper. Stuck to the facts. But the facts were bad enough. You couldn't avoid the sleaze. It was all there. In the evidence. It didn't need any extra hype. And as for destroying lives . . . hadn't the men done that for themselves?

'We'll report the trial, when it starts,' said Fiona, slowly. 'That's all. But I can't speak for other papers. It might even make the nationals. You know that, don't you?'

'You're all as bad,' yelled Mrs Hall, banging her fist on the desk. 'You know that, don't you? Trial by media! He'll be guilty no matter what the jury decides. Our lives are already ruined. And he won't be able to stand it, I know he won't. I'm sure he'll try to . . .'

She stopped abruptly, turned and walked towards the door. She opened it, then looked back at Fiona.

'As if you care!' she snapped. 'As far as you're concerned it would just be another good story, wouldn't it? If he killed himself?'

Fiona shook her head, sighed and looked up at the clock as Mrs Hall stormed from the room. Almost midday. She had a meeting in five minutes. Just time to return Debra's call. She must remember to ask how poor Miriam got on, whether Tim had turned up at the school on time and whether he'd been sober.

Chapter 2

'Do you girls want a lift or what?' said Tonya's mother standing in the doorway.

She didn't comment on the state of the bedroom. The rejected clothes, the make-up and the shoes scattered round the floor. She didn't even mention the hair dye that had somehow missed Beth's head, splattering the bedroom walls. Tonya's mum never fussed. She was only 38. With her short top showing off her glossy, dark skin and navel ring, she looked more like Tonya's twin than her mother. And she was in on all their secrets.

'Don't forget,' Beth told her, as the three girls eventually clambered into the car, 'if my parents phone, tell them I'm in the loo or something. And I'll phone them back. Same for Debs.'

Debra was fairly sure her parents wouldn't phone. OK, so they were completely paranoid about their 'positions' and how embarrassing it would be if either she or Lori got into any major bother, which made it difficult to be totally truthful with them sometimes. But they weren't quite so suspicious as Beth's mum and step-dad. If Debra said it was a small party at Tonya's, then that's what they'd believe.

'I don't know why you don't just tell them!' Debra's sister, Lori, had said. 'They won't mind you going to the pub. Not for a GCSE party. Not if you're honest about it.'

16

'Just like you're honest about everything you get up to at Uni?' Debra had asked.

'That's different,' Lori had said. 'They're not likely to find out, are they? But Dad's sure to hear about this. The whole flaming year group's going by the sound of it! Then you'll get the lecture about trust and letting them down.'

'Yeah, well, I'll deal with it when it happens,' Debra had said.

She didn't want to run the risk of them stopping her. And, however delighted they'd been by her results, they might if they knew the party was at The Lion. Benny and Tonya had booked the room for an alleged 18th birthday party so there'd be no hassle about drinking. But they needn't have bothered. The Lion, in a quiet spot a few miles out of town, was notorious. Well known for its late hours and lax standards. Not to mention the regular fights that broke out.

Every so often the cops would turn up and run a half-hearted sort of check. Hopefully they wouldn't choose tonight for one of their visits. 'Deputy Head's daughter in pub raid drama' wasn't the sort of headline Mum would want for her paper.

'Turn left,' Beth suddenly squealed. 'We're picking up Miriam, remember?'

'She won't be there,' said Tonya, as the car whipped round the corner. 'She only said it to shut you up. She's got no intention of going.'

But there Miriam was, standing by her gate, next to the

'Sold' sign. Wearing jeans and a baggy tee shirt. Not exactly glammed-up.

'I'm only staying a couple of hours,' she informed them. 'My cousin'll be coming past around ten so he's going to stop and pick me up.'

The mention of Miriam's cousin hung in the car, waiting for comment. If things had been bad for Miriam since the trial, what must it have been like for Eddie?

'How is he?' said Beth. 'How's he doing?'

'Not bad,' said Miriam. 'Doesn't say much. But then, Eddie never does. Mum's tried to talk to him, get him to open up a bit, but he won't. And I can't really blame him. It doesn't do any good to keep going over it, like Mum does. Looking for explanations, excuses! Her and Dad arguing about it all the time. Going round in circles.'

'What about Eddie's mother?' said Tonya. 'Don't suppose she's been in touch.'

Miriam shook her head.

'Last time they heard from her Eddie was only ten. No one knows where she is or even whether she's still alive. Uncle Gordon was all Eddie really had and now...'

Miriam lapsed into silence, the tears starting to fall.

'Well if you change your mind,' said Tonya's mum brightly. 'About leaving early, you can always come back to ours with the rest of them.'

'Yeah,' said Beth. 'Then tomorrow we're gonna go into town.'

'Have lunch,' Tonya added.

'See a film,' said Debra, determined to join in, lightening the mood.

It worked. They were off. Girls on a celebratory night out. Chattering. Making plans for the last week or so of the holiday. Unaware that someone was making plans of quite a different sort.

It was the picture that gave me the idea. At least I think it was. Sitting there at the top of the front page, above the story of the latest porn trial. The feel-good factor pic. Drawing attention away from all the sleaze, the nastiness.

It was a good photo. Very good. All the clever girls, the pretty girls. And her, of course. Debra Cardew. Editor's daughter. Right at the front.

Best results ever, the story said. Eighty-three per cent of pupils got five or more A-C grades. Thirteen kids got straight As. Omar Choudhray had one of the five best maths results in the country, the article said. And where was he? At the back! With the other lad. Hidden behind half a dozen girls. 'Cos the paper has to give the readers what they want, doesn't it? The eye-candy. The short skirts and tight tops.

She looks so pleased with herself, Debra. Smug. Like the rest of her family. With their nice, neat, perfect little lives. They think they're so good. So superior. Looking down on everyone.

Well, it got me thinking, didn't it? Bet Mummy and Daddy are dead proud of Debra. And if anything was to happen to her . . . well, that would shake them up a bit, wouldn't it?

I mean, what if . . .

★

19

The girls pushed their way through the crowded bar to the back room where the party was taking place. It was unusually hot for the end of August and the pub was already stuffy, heavy with cigarette smoke. Debra peered through the haze, scanning the tables and the small dance floor for Marc. He wasn't there.

'We'll never get served in here,' said Beth, looking at the tangle round the tiny corner bar. 'We'll have more chance out there. Want do you want?'

What Debra wanted was to look for Marc so she followed Beth and kept watch on the main door while Beth tried to catch the barman's eye.

'Oh no,' said Debra, as three people walked in. 'Beth, are you served yet?'

'Nearly. Why?'

'It's super-creep,' Debra hissed. 'Lori's ex. Oh, shit. Too late. He's coming over... Hi, Stefan.'

'Hello, Debra. How you doing? Saw your picture in the paper. All As, same as Lori, was it?'

Five seconds, Debra thought. Five seconds it had taken him to get onto Lori. He was slipping. He could usually manage it in less than three.

'How is she?' Stefan asked, taking on the mournful look of an abandoned dog.

'About the same as she was last week when you asked me,' Debra said.

'She's still at home, is she?'

'Yeah. She might go away for a week at the beginning of September, before she goes back to Uni though.

Depends how much money she manages to save.'

Whoops. Bit of a mistake. Debra knew exactly what the next question would be.

'Away? Where to?'

'Er, not sure. She'll get one of those last minute package deals I expect.'

'It's OK,' said Stefan, smiling. 'I'm not going to follow her or anything! I'm over it, now. Completely over it. Like Lori says, you have to move on, don't you?'

'Yeah,' said Debra, snatching a couple of drinks off Beth.

'I mean, it was gonna happen, anyway,' Stefan said. 'Thanks to your dad. He never liked me, did he? I mean, I reckon that's why Lori finished with me. 'Cos your dad kept on about that dope business.'

'Yeah, you're probably right,' Debra said.

Dad had certainly gone ballistic when he'd caught Lori and Stefan smoking dope in their garage. He'd gone on about it for ages. Even threatened to call the cops if it happened again. He'd blamed Stefan, of course. Which was dead right 'cos Lori never usually touched drugs. And if Stefan wanted to believe Lori dumped him just to get Dad off her case, then who was Debra to argue?

'Tell Lori I was asking about her, will you?' Stefan said, slouching off.

No chance, thought Debra.

'Doesn't sound like he's over her,' said Beth as they made their way back to the party room. 'They've been finished ages though, haven't they?'

'Over a year,' said Debra. 'They split up just before she

started Uni. She didn't want any ties. And it was never that serious with Stefan. Not for Lori.'

'He's good looking,' said Beth, her eyes following him. 'Dead fit.'

'Yeah,' said Debra. 'But he's a bit of a nutter. Jealous sort. Didn't like her seeing her friends and stuff. Lori just used to laugh it off,' she added, shuddering. 'But I thought it was a bit creepy. I was glad when she dumped him.'

They handed the drinks over to Tonya and Miriam. Five minutes later Miriam had an empty glass and was heading back to the bar. An hour later, she'd had six drinks to their two and was happily getting off with Omar on the edge of the dance floor.

'It's so hot in here,' Debra said. 'I think I'll go outside for a minute.'

'For the fifth time tonight!' said Beth. 'He's not gonna come, you know. No matter how many times you look.'

'Twice,' said Debra. 'I've been out twice. Because I'm hot. Not because I'm looking for Marc. And you don't need to come with me. I don't need a chaperone.'

She walked out through the bar, not even noticing the man sitting in the corner, watching her. The man put down his drink and prepared to follow.

I admit it was all a fantasy at first. A pleasant little daydream. Debra Cardew goes missing. Like teenage girls do sometimes. Has she finally cracked under the pressure of being so bloody perfect? Run away? Topped herself? Had she been exchanging mail with some nasty man on the net? Gone to meet him? Was she abducted? Was it someone she knew? Or some nutter striking at random? Is she dead or is there still hope?

Not knowing. That's what would drive the family mad, isn't it? I could see them making one of those televised pleas for Debra to come home.

'You won't be in any trouble, Debra. Just get in touch. Just come home.'

But she wouldn't be able to, would she?

Then I got to thinking. It wouldn't be that difficult, would it? Waiting for a time when she was walking home alone. Maybe when she'd had a bit too much to drink. Or perhaps if something had been slipped into her drink . . .

It's not difficult to get hold of stuff like that. Even in a smallish town like this. Not if you know where to look. You can even get stuff on prescription. If you're having trouble sleeping.

So I started to have a think, make a few preparations, didn't I? I wasn't going to rush into it. Maybe I wouldn't do anything at all. It was a crazy idea. Completely crazy. I could see that.

But once I'd got the idea in my head, it wouldn't go away. Besides, it wouldn't do any harm to think about it, would it? Maybe watch her. Wait for a chance.

As Debra stepped out of the pub, Marc's brother's car sped into the front car park. There was no mistaking it. Bright, metallic green with black markings. Fancied himself as a bit of a boy racer, did Dean Cavendish. He'd supposedly calmed down a lot since he was excluded from school a few years back. He'd had some sort of 'anger management' therapy and got himself a joiners'

23

apprenticeship, which he loved. But he was still a complete idiot behind the wheel of a car.

There were no empty spaces out the front so the car spun round and Debra tried to see if Marc was in the passenger seat. He wasn't. As the car zipped past her and headed round the back, she could see there was only one person in it. The driver. And the driver was Marc.

'Shit!' said Debra.

Where the hell was Dean? There was no way he'd let anyone drive that car. Let alone an under-aged driver with no licence and no insurance. Marc must have taken it! He was mad. Completely mad.

He'd also been drinking. That was obvious from the moment he ran back round the corner and bounded up to her.

'Hey, Debs!' he said, grabbing her and kissing her.

'Marc,' she managed to say, when he finally let go. 'What are you doing?'

'Why? Don't you like it?' he said, trying to kiss her again.

She did like it. Far too much. No one could make her feel quite so good, quite so quickly as Marc, but she resisted the temptation to hurl herself at him.

'I don't mean that,' said Debra, pushing him gently away. 'I mean the car!'

'What car?' he said, grinning.

'The car you were driving, Marc! Dean's car.'

'You pissed already, Debs?' he said. 'I wasn't driving no car. That was Dean. He gave me a lift.'

24

Debra stared at him for a moment, doubting the evidence of her own senses. Marc was such a good liar. A real professional.

'Where is he now then?' she said.

'Sitting in the car, tinkering with the sound system. Go and look if you don't believe me.'

He leant forward and kissed her again, before strolling into the pub. Debra wondered whether to go and check. But she knew there was no need. The look of innocence on his face, the sincerity in his voice, didn't mean a thing. She'd seen it all too often to be taken in. Marc had been driving that car. She was sure of it. And there was no way she could let him drive it again. Somehow she had to get the keys off him.

She turned to follow him into the pub but the minute she stepped through the door someone grabbed her and pulled her back outside.

'Where the heck's Debs got to?' Beth asked Tonya.

'I dunno, but Marc's just walked in. Let's ask if he's seen her.'

'Yeah, she was outside,' Marc said. 'I thought she was gonna follow me in but when I turned round, she was going back out again with some bloke.'

'Who?' said Beth. 'Which bloke?'

'I dunno, do I? Sort of middle-aged bloke, I think. Bit scruffy looking.'

Beth and Tonya pushed past him and made their way through the bar. Even before they got outside they

25

could hear the shouting.

'A written warning! I'm on a written warning now, thanks to you. Why did you do it, Debs? Why did you have to tell her? I wasn't even drunk!'

'I've told you, Tim, I didn't tell Mum anything,' Debra was saying as Beth and Tonya appeared at her side. 'She asked me and I said you were fine. Honest!'

'Well somebody did! Somebody told her I turned up at your school pissed.'

'It could have been anyone,' said Beth quietly. 'There were loads of teachers around. And it was pretty obvious!'

'Who asked you? This is between me and Debs.'

'No it isn't,' said Beth. 'It's got nothing to do with her. She's coming in. Come on, Debra.'

'It's OK,' said Debra. 'How did you know I'd be here tonight, Tim?'

'I didn't,' said Tim. 'I was just having a drink. Saw you walk through. You don't think I was stalking you or anything, do you?'

'Don't be daft,' said Debra. ''Course not. And I'm sorry about what's happened. But it wasn't me. I didn't say anything. I swear.'

'Yeah,' said Tim. 'I'm sorry, too. It's not your fault, Debs. You can't help having a complete cow of a mother. You should have heard her going on at me. Like I was a bloody school kid or something.'

He sat down at one of the outside tables, his head in his hands.

'She doesn't know what it's like,' he was muttering to

26

himself. 'To lose someone. She doesn't understand.'

'She does,' Debra said, as Beth tried to pull her away. 'You know she's tried to help! But you won't let her. What about that doctor she wants you to see?'

'Doctor!' Tim said, looking up and staring at them out of bloodshot eyes. 'Doctor! What do they know? What did they do for Evie? Made her wait six months to see a bloody consultant. Left it till it was too late. They killed her. Do you know what it's like, watching someone die like that? No, of course you don't. But they'll pay for their bloody incompetence. I'm going to sue. They won't get away with it.'

'Come in, Debs,' said Beth, as Tim's head sunk into his hands again. 'You can't do anything.'

'Yes, that's right,' said Tim, getting unsteadily to his feet. 'Go back to your party, Debs. Enjoy yourself. While you still can. I'm going home.'

'Who was Evie?' asked Tonya as the girls went back inside. 'His wife?'

'Well, his partner,' Debra said. 'They were going to get married, I think. But she died back in March. She had cancer.'

She didn't tell them the whole story. It was Tim's business. It was private. And she felt a strange sort of loyalty to Tim. Out of all the people on the paper, he was the one who'd always been really nice to her. Made a fuss of her. Talked to her whenever she was hanging round the office waiting for Mum. He liked kids, Mum said, even though he didn't have any of his own.

Debra paused, letting Beth and Tonya push their way through the crowds. It didn't seem fair somehow, the way life seemed to dump on some people for no apparent reason. Tim's wife had been killed in a car accident, years ago, before he ever came to work on the paper. But he'd obviously loved her a lot. Kept her picture on his desk.

One or two of the women at work had been interested in Tim, Mum had said. But he hadn't bothered with relationships. Not for ages. Not until he met Evie. Then just as things started to get serious, Evie got sick.

It wasn't, though, the cancer that had killed her. She'd taken an overdose. In the final stages. And there was something else. Something Tim had let slip one Saturday when Debra had bumped into him in town, pissed out of his head. Something she'd never told anyone. But, on reflection, maybe she should have done. Maybe this wasn't something Tim could get through on his own.

'Hey, Debra,' a whining voice said, as she headed back towards the party. 'Will you give this note to Lori?'

'No, Stefan, I bloody well won't,' said Debra. 'Just leave her alone. It's over.'

'Bitch!' yelled Stefan, as a couple of middle-aged women turned to stare.

One of them held Debra's gaze for a moment, as though it was somehow Debra's fault that Stefan was ranting and swearing. The woman's face looked vaguely familiar. Hopefully not a friend of Mum's. Someone who might tell.

'Look at the state of them,' the woman muttered to her friend. 'Half dressed, plastered in make-up!'

'Come on!' said Beth, grabbing Debra's hand. 'Safira says Miriam's puking up in the loo. Let's go and sort her out! I thought he was going?'

Debra half turned to see Tim walking back into the pub. She couldn't help worrying about him. She thought about going back to talk to him but Beth was already dragging her into the party.

In the corner, near the narrow corridor which led to the ladies' loo, Debra caught sight of Marc. His head buried in Amy Parker's chest, his hand creeping up her skirt. Amy bloody Parker of all people!

'That's it!' Debra announced. 'I've had enough. I'm going home.'

Chapter 3

'I'm fine now,' said Miriam, knocking back another drink. 'Leave me alone. I want to dance.'

She took a couple of steps before crashing into Debra and Beth, shrieking with laughter as she fell. Debra sighed. Beth had persuaded her not to go home but she wasn't exactly having a fun-packed evening, especially as the last half hour had been spent in the ladies, cleaning up after Miriam! Well, at least Miriam was happy now, Debra thought, as she lifted her up again. Miriam laughing wasn't something that happened often these days.

'It's all right,' said a voice, as a man in his mid twenties, wearing clothes that looked as though they belonged to someone much older, strolled up to them. 'I'll take her home.'

'Don't want to go home, Eddie,' Miriam said. 'I've changed my mind. I'm gonna stay at Tonya's. With my mates.'

Miriam linked arms with Beth and Debra and started giggling. Several people were glancing in their direction, Debra noticed. Because of Miriam? Unlikely. There were plenty of people in a worse state than her. More likely they were looking at Eddie. He glared back at them, defiantly, and they turned away.

Debra didn't know Eddie Wilcox very well. Barely at all, in fact. Not many people did. Eddie had been at a private boys' school before going on to university. Then he'd gone off travelling for a while, Miriam said, before coming back to work for his dad's property development company about eighteen months ago. He seemed fairly quiet. Nondescript. The sort of person who blended into their surroundings. So, back then, no one would have recognized him. But now they did. Because of what his dad had done.

'Come on, Miriam,' Eddie was saying, quietly, patiently. 'Let me take you home.'

He was shorter than Miriam. Dark-haired. A touch overweight. They obviously got their genes from completely different sides of their family, Debra thought. Apart from the green eyes. Miriam's now bright and fiery. Eddie's tired and vacant.

'Not going,' said Miriam, lurching in the general direction of Omar Choudhray. 'Going to dance.'

Eddie shrugged as Omar caught Miriam and steered her onto the dance floor.

'I can't make her go,' Eddie said. 'But will you keep an eye on her? Make sure she gets back all right?'

'Sure,' said Beth.

'Right,' said Eddie. 'I'll wait in the bar for half an hour or so, in case she changes her mind.'

'Beth, my darling!' someone yelled, turning everyone's attention to the dance floor.

Benny, the class clown, had dropped to his knees and was sliding towards them, his hands held out.

'Come and dance with me,' he pleaded.

'Idiot,' Beth grinned, pulling him to his feet.

She wandered off, leaving Debra staring after her, wondering whether to go and join Tonya and the large group of girls gyrating around in the middle. She was about to move when arms clasped her round her waist and a warm mouth started nibbling her ear.

'Guess who?' Marc whispered.

Debra wriggled round to face him.

'You look fantastic tonight, Debs,' he said. 'Yum!'

'Where's Amy?' she asked, knowing Marc's words and kisses didn't always mean very much.

'Gone to the loo,' said Marc, pulling her closer. 'Thank God. Couldn't get away from her. She grabbed me the minute I walked in.'

'And forced you to stick your hand up her skirt, I suppose?' Debra snapped.

He grinned, by way of an answer and, before Debra could stop him, he was kissing her again, his breath tasting of beer, reminding her of something she needed to do. She returned his kiss, her hands sliding round his back, down onto his jeans, her fingers slipping gently into his pocket, groping, searching.

'Hey, what you doing?' he said, pushing her away, just before she could grab the car keys.

'Nothing,' she said.

'I'm not gonna drive it home, OK?' said Marc, abandoning his earlier claims of innocence. 'Our Dean let me bring it. He's coming over with his mate, later. He's driving back. So don't go saying anything to anyone, right?'

Debra didn't believe him. Somehow she'd get those keys off him by the end of the night. Or maybe she wouldn't have to. Someone had just stormed in. And by the look on his face, he hadn't known about Marc borrowing the car at all.

'Oh shit,' said Marc, catching sight of Dean. 'Sorry, Debs. Gotta go.'

Debra stood, shaking her head, as she watched Marc trying to sidle out of the room. She saw Dean grab his arm and push him against the wall. Well at least he'd succeeded in doing what she'd failed to do. He'd taken the keys out of Marc's pocket.

'Hey, Debs,' shouted Tonya. 'Why aren't you dancing? You look like a right loner.'

Could tonight be the night? Could I get that lucky so soon? With everybody drunk. Or pretending to be drunk, in some cases. Debra's spending a lot of time on her own. Shouldn't be difficult to lure her away. That's how they work, isn't it? Predators. Isolate the one they want away from the herd. Then pounce.

The trick is to keep cool.

But it's not that easy. Knowing I might never get a better chance. It'd help if she had a bit more to drink. Or put her glass down again so I could move things along a bit. The place is so crowded, no one would notice. As long as I was careful.

If there was a problem, I could pull back at any stage, couldn't I? And if there wasn't? If I manage to get her out of here?

I'm not sure. I'm not sure I'm ready. Haven't had chance to think it all out properly. Not sure I want to go ahead at all, really. So why did I bring the stuff then?

I must have been planning to use it, mustn't I? But no. Even if I got her drugged up, I'd never get her out of here without someone noticing, would I? Unless . . .

'Fancy a drink?' Marc asked.

'You're still alive then?' said Debra. 'Where's Dean?'

'Nipped out to check his precious car but he might get a bit of a surprise later,' he said, dangling a key in front of her face.

'Marc!'

'Spare one,' he said. 'Idiot keeps it in the glove compartment. Don't worry. I'm not gonna drive home. Just thought I might hide the car. Wind him up a bit. Now d'yer want a drink or not?'

'Yeah,' said Debra. 'I think I need one.'

'You'll have to get them, I'm out of money,' said Marc, as Amy Parker headed towards them. 'Er, let's go to the other bar.'

She went because she was worried about him, Debra told herself. Wanted to keep her eye on him. To make sure he didn't slip off and try to drive home.

There were loads of people in the bar who she knew. She waved at a few of them, including Tim, but his eyes were firmly fixed on his drink. From the back table, near the window, Debra could feel Stefan's puppy-dog gaze. Willing her to transform magically into Lori, probably. Dean had just stomped back in. And, from the doorway

34

that led into the party room, another pair of eyes, staring. Amy Parker.

Debra suddenly shivered.

'You OK?' said Marc, taking her drink off her and putting it on the table beside them.

'Yeah, fine,' she said, as he wrapped his arms round her and started rubbing her shoulders. 'Someone just walked over my grave, as Mum might say.'

'Er, I don't suppose,' Marc said, suddenly sounding clear and sober, 'that your dad's said anything, has he? About what happened at school on Thursday?'

'He mentioned it, yeah,' said Debra.

He hadn't of course. Dad hardly ever talked about school business when she was around. Especially stuff about other pupils. But Marc wasn't to know that.

'He said he thought he'd gone a bit over the top with you and if you wanted to come back to sixth form—'

'Nah,' said Marc, dropping his arms and moving away from her. 'Mum says I should. And Mr Mason. But Dean reckons I'm better off out of it. Besides I've got a place at college now. Went to see 'em yesterday and they offered me a place straight away.'

'Same college as me,' said Amy, suddenly appearing and grabbing Marc's arm. 'Marc's going to the same college as me! School's for kids.'

Amy giggled, making Debra wonder what Marc saw in her. She was also rubbing her hand up and down Marc's leg, hinting at exactly where the attraction lay. Marc wasn't exactly fighting her off.

'Was Daddy pleased with you then, Debs?' said Amy, deliberately winding things up. 'No problem with *your* sixth form place I bet.'

'No,' said Debra, turning away.

She hated Amy Parker. Debra had been asked to look after Amy when she'd joined their junior school in Year 4. And she had done. Even though Amy, with her constant attention seeking, hadn't been exactly popular, Debra had made sure people included her, accepted her. Amy had settled down a lot and they'd become friends. Or so Debra had thought.

But once they'd got to seniors Amy had been put in lower sets. Found some new friends. Turned on Debra. Made her life a misery in Year 7. Even worse in Year 8 for a while, when Amy's bullying had turned physical. Nudges in the corridor. Heavy bags accidentally crashing into Debra's stomach when no one was looking.

Heaven knows how long it would have gone on for if Lori hadn't stepped in and sorted it out. And that was the trouble really. Big sister had sorted it. Not Debra. And though Debra had learnt to ignore and avoid Amy, she'd never really learnt to deal with her. Not on Amy's terms.

'Saw your picture in *Mummy's* paper,' said Amy. 'It was quite good. Didn't make you look too fat. And that spot on your neck hardly showed up at all. Or is it a new one? It looks ever so red, Debs. You ought to put something on it.'

'Yeah well,' said Debra. 'At least my problem can be solved with a bit of cream.'

'Meaning?' said Amy.

Debra half turned away, sorry she'd let herself get drawn in.

'No, come on, Miss Perfect Pants,' said Amy, releasing her hold on Marc to grab Debra's arm. 'What do you mean?'

Debra told her.

It was brilliant. Once those two started bitching and sniping at each other, stage one was easy, wasn't it? Slipping something into Debra's drink. Because quite a few people had moved in closer. Some had drifted out of the party, forming a semi-circle. Grinning at each other, wondering how serious it was going to get. Would the nails come out?

Hopefully not because that would spoil everything, wouldn't it? If Debra got thrown out of the pub before she could finish her drink. And I thought she might. She was really going for it. You wouldn't think a girl like Debra even knew all those words.

'And you know what, Amy?' she finished. 'You and Marc deserve each other. You're welcome to him.'

'Ooooooh,' said Amy, as Debra picked up her drink, pushed her way through the crowds and marched off.

Careless, see. Girls are told not to put their drinks down. Not to leave them lying around. But most of them don't bother. They never think it's going to happen to them. People round here are far too trusting. I mean, there's jackets and bags lying about all over the place. A pick-pocket's playground. Which gives me another idea. Something to do while I'm waiting.

Then it's a case of keeping calm. Keeping a low profile. Nothing's going to happen for a while. Though it's hard to tell.

I slipped two in, just to be sure. But it'll depend how much she's had to drink. What she's eaten. What sort of mood she's in. Half an hour, maybe, for the first effects to kick in. An hour or so before she starts to lose it completely.

Mustn't get too wound up. Mustn't get careless. A million things could happen. And I daren't make a move unless it's safe. Absolutely safe.

Maybe I ought to leave for a while? Make a show of it. Let someone notice me going home. Then slip back in. Or maybe it's better to stay put. Talk to people. Move around. The party room's filling up. Loads of people are drifting through from the bar. It should be easy enough to keep an eye on her. From a distance. Wait until the effects start to show. Hope her friends don't get to her before I do.

'I got you another drink,' said Tonya. 'You deserve it after the way you laid into Amy. It was brill! I've never seen Amy speechless before. Pity Beth missed it. She's in the loo again with Miriam.'

'Thanks,' said Debra, swigging back the contents of her glass and starting on the bottle Tonya had given her. 'What time is it?'

'Almost eleven.'

'Eleven o'clock?' said Debra. 'And I haven't even had time to dance yet! Come on.'

'You OK?' said Tonya as they wandered onto the dance floor.

'Yeah, why?'

'About Marc, I meant?'

38

'Yeah, I reckon,' said Debra.

'Did you hear him mouthing off to Benny earlier? About your dad? He said your dad's got it in for him. Ever since that business with Dean and—'

'No,' said Debra. 'Don't tell me anymore. I'm sick of it. I don't care. I don't want to know.'

She was surprised to find she meant it. She didn't care. She really didn't care. If Marc wanted to go to college, let him. Let him hide Dean's car or drive it home. Let him kill himself. Why should it bother her? She felt good. She was going to enjoy herself. Like you're supposed to do on a night out. Like everyone else was doing.

Word of the party had got round. Apart from all the Year 11s, there was a group of girls from Year 10. A dozen or so sixth formers. A few ex-pupils. Even some of the younger teachers – Miss Lewis, Mr Khan and Allan Mason, happily turning a blind eye to all the under-age drinking. Her dad, Debra thought, would go ballistic if he knew.

Mr Mason smiled at her. But it wasn't a friendly smile. It was the sort of patronizing smile he used to give her in history lessons, immediately before some sarcastic put-down. He was like that, Mr Mason. Either he liked you or he didn't. Debra wasn't sure why he disliked *her* so much. Probably 'cos of Dad. There'd been another bust-up on Thursday. About Marc. She'd overheard Dad telling Mum about it.

'Three years,' he'd said. 'Three years Allan's been teaching and thinks he knows everything!'

Dad had said a whole lot more but she wasn't going to think about it now. She was supposed to be celebrating and all she'd done was think about other people's problems!

'Steady,' said Tonya, as Debra's dancing got wilder. 'You nearly knocked me out then.'

'I don't care!' said Debra, dancing off on her own. 'I'm having fun.'

She was also attracting a fair bit of attention. Not least from three lads from the lower sixth who were leaning against the wall watching her. One of them smiled at her, waiting for a response. He wasn't particularly good looking. Not like Marc. But he had nice eyes. She smiled back, luring him towards her.

'OK if I join you?' he asked, shuffling around, out of time with the music.

Not exactly a natural mover.

'Simon,' he said. 'I was on the Paris trip with you, last year. Remember?'

Debra didn't. Paris was memorable because that's when she'd first got together with Marc. But she smiled and nodded anyway.

'Won't your boyfriend mind?' he asked. 'Me dancing with you?'

'Haven't got a boyfriend,' she said.

'Good,' said Simon, taking hold of her hands as he danced. 'That's good.'

It *was* good. Maybe the evening was going to be all right after all. Simon was nice. Sort of funny. And sweet.

40

Said he'd wanted to ask her out for ages. Only he didn't think he stood a chance. Not with someone as pretty and popular as her. Not with Marc Cavendish around.

Simon was saying something now but she couldn't make out what it was. His voice was going all weird. Fading in and out, like a dodgy radio. His face was going weird too. All sort of furry and blurry. And her headache was getting worse. At first she'd hardly realized it was there. It had started off as a gentle throb, pounding to the beat of the music. Getting more intense as the lights started. Lights behind her eyes. Or was that the disco lights? Flashing, swirling, making patterns on the floor which made her dizzy. And sick. Mustn't throw up. Not on Marc. No, not Marc. It was Simon. She was with Simon.

'Sorry,' she said, pulling away, leaving him standing there, bemused.

She made her way off the dance floor, stumbling into the couple by the wall. At least she'd thought it was a couple but, as her eyes started to focus, she realized it was two girls.

'Miriam's just puked on my shoes,' Beth was saying. 'Oh, Debs, not you as well? You look terrible.'

'Feel telliful,' said Debra. 'And snick.'

'Let me get Miriam sorted out,' said Beth, as Debra bolted towards the ladies. 'Then I'll be with you.'

'Oh God,' Debra groaned, sinking to her knees inside the cubicle.

She hadn't had that much to drink, had she? She didn't know. Could barely remember. A couple of glasses of wine before the party. The party at Tonya's. No the party wasn't at Tonya's. It was in a pub and it wasn't very nice. People kept being mean to her. And it wasn't her fault.

Her stomach was doing somersaults. She was hot. Far too hot. Where was Beth? Beth said she'd come but she hadn't.

Mixing her drinks. That was the problem. Stand up. Head for the sink. Where were the taps? Why wouldn't they turn? Not that sort of tap. OK, splash face with cold water. Don't pass out. Want to get back. To Simon. Nice Simon. Sink won't stay still. Not fair. Keeps moving about. Face all funny. Make-up smudged. And the floor's moving. Round and round and round and . . . got to get out. Got to get to bed. Lie down. Need to lie down. Legs won't work. Silly. Mum, help me. I don't feel well. Cold now. So very cold. Beth? Mum? Where is everybody? Turn those lights off. Somebody. Stop the lights. That's better. See the door now. Too heavy. Won't open. Don't want to stay here. Too hot again. Pull. No push. Sick. Feel sick. And hot. Burning. Sleep. Lie down. Just let me lie down. Air. That's better. Cold air.

Debra turned right, towards the cold breeze, not left, back the party. She stumbled towards the emergency exit and headed outside. Exactly as the person who'd left the door open had hoped she would.

Chapter 4

Beth rushed out of the pub towards Tonya's car, hoping Debra would be waiting. She wasn't.

'I can't find her,' Beth told Tonya's mum. 'I can't find Debs anywhere.'

'She'll turn up in a minute,' said Tonya's mum. 'Miriam's looking round the back. She said she fancied a bit of a walk to sober up! And Tonya's gone back to check the party room.'

'I've told you, she's not there!' said Beth, trying to keep the panic out of her voice. 'She's not anywhere. And when I phoned, her phone rang out. In her bag. Under a table.'

'OK,' said Tonya's mum, taking the bag that Beth was holding out to her. 'So she won't have gone far, will she? Not without this. Now tell me again. When was the last time anyone saw her?'

'I'm not sure,' said Beth. 'She wasn't feeling too good. She went to the ladies but by the time I'd settled Miriam, Debs had gone. I thought she'd be dancing or something so I didn't bother . . . until people started to drift off and I couldn't see her.'

'Well it's no big mystery, is it?' said Amy Parker, whose taxi had just pulled up. 'I mean Marc disappeared a while ago, didn't he? Bit of a coincidence I'd say.'

'She wouldn't just go off like that,' said Beth. 'Not even with Marc. Not without saying.'

'Yeah, right,' said Amy, getting into her taxi. 'I just wish he'd make his mind up, that's all. The two-timing bastard!'

She slammed the door and as the taxi drove off, Beth saw Tonya coming towards them, shaking her head.

'Nobody's seen her,' said Tonya. 'Not for ages. But I've asked the landlady to check upstairs. In case Debs wandered up there and crashed out on their bed or something.'

Beth looked at her watch. They were supposed to meet up half an hour ago. It wasn't like Debs. It wasn't like her at all.

'We need to do something,' said Beth. 'Phone the police.'

'We'll look a bit stupid,' said Tonya, 'if she's curled up asleep or something.'

'I don't care,' said Beth. 'I don't care how stupid we . . .'

She stopped as Miriam came running round the corner, breathing heavily, clutching something in her hand.

'I found this,' she said, holding up a black shoe. 'By the fire exit. I think it's Debra's.'

Beth snatched the shoe, willing it to be someone else's. Anyone else's. But it wasn't. It was Debra's. Beth was sure of it.

'That's it!' said Beth. 'We're phoning the cops. Now!'

'Hang on,' said Tonya's mum. 'She's maybe gone home.'

'Without her bag?' said Beth. 'With only one shoe?'

'She probably kicked both of them off,' said Tonya's mum. 'And forgot all about the bag. I've done it myself, when I've been drunk. Let me just try her parents.'

Beth paced up and down as Tonya's mum made the call. She heard her trying to explain, muttering apologies into the phone.

'No, not our house. The Lion. Yes, that one. Yes, I did know. I'm sorry. I said I'm sorry! Look, I'm sure she'll be OK. We'll find her. Yes, of course.'

'What's going on?' shouted the landlord, storming out of the pub. 'Someone reckons a girl's gone missing. You're not phoning the cops, are you?'

'*I'm* not,' said Tonya's mum. 'The girl's mother's going to. Her dad's on his way over.'

The landlord snarled a single expletive followed by 'bloody kids' before storming back inside. Minutes later he was back, herding the few remaining drinkers and party-goers off the premises.

'Hang on,' said Beth. 'The police might want to talk to people.'

'Yeah,' he snapped. 'That's what I'm worried about.'

'Not about a missing sixteen-year-old?' said Tonya's mother.

'She'll turn up,' said the landlord, shrugging. 'They always do.'

It was so easy. So incredibly easy. She virtually passed out in my arms. The minute she got outside. Didn't turn round. Didn't shout out. Didn't seem to care who'd caught her.

All the plans I'd made. What I was going to do, what I was going to say if things started to go wrong . . . well, I didn't need them, did I? I just lifted her up and carried her. That was the hardest part really. She felt a lot heavier than she looks. A dead weight, as they say.

One of her shoes fell off but that didn't matter. I didn't have time to stop. Needed to get her out of the way before anyone saw anything. But if anyone had, if anyone had come out, well I was ready to abort operations, wasn't I? Say she'd fainted. Which was true in a way. And that I was taking her back inside or something.

They haven't got any security cameras or anything. It's the last thing they'd want at The Lion. And nobody saw me. I'm sure of that. Because I was looking around all the time, wasn't I? But if the worst comes to the worst, I've got it covered. I reckon if anyone spotted me, the police will be onto me straight away. Within the next hour. And if they are, then I just hand Debra over, don't I? Make out like I was looking after her. Say I found her wandering about. I mean, Debra's not going to argue, is she? The state she's in she's not going to remember anything.

Which is good. Because I don't want to hurt her. I've got nothing against Debra. Not really. Hurting Debra isn't the idea at all. I just need to keep her out of the way for a while.

Beth sat in the bar with her parents.

'I don't understand,' her mother was saying. 'What on earth were you doing here in the first place? You said you were going to Tonya's. This is what happens when you lie all the time!'

'Don't!' Beth screamed. 'Don't start lecturing me. Not now! Debra's missing. Don't you think I feel bad enough without you going on at me?'

'It's all right,' said her step-dad, putting his arm round her, as she started to cry. 'I'm going to ask if we can take you home now.'

'I don't want to go,' said Beth. 'I don't want to go anywhere. Not until they find Debs.'

'It's not going to help,' said her step-dad. 'Just sitting here. You've given your statement. There's nothing else you can do.'

Statement, Beth thought. There was something about her statement that wasn't right. Something she hadn't explained properly. But she couldn't remember. Couldn't think straight. Besides, it didn't really matter. Any minute now someone would ring in and say they'd found her. They had to. Nothing bad could happen to Debs.

Those sorts of things happened in other places, to other people. The police had hinted as much themselves, when the first couple of uniformed cops had turned up. When they'd seemed as if they weren't going to take it seriously at all. Sixteen-year-old girl wanders off from party. Happens all the time. Only this wasn't any sixteen-year-old. This was Debra. Debra wouldn't do anything like that. As Beth had told them, over and over.

Not that it had made any difference. The police had latched on to the rotten night Debs had been having. The argument with Amy. The boyfriend trouble. Tim. Stefan. They reckoned she'd probably had enough. Taken herself off somewhere. And they hadn't really lurched into action until Debra's dad had arrived. Beth wasn't sure what Mr Cardew had said but it had certainly made a difference.

47

Beth looked over to where Mr Cardew was standing with a couple of men who were almost certainly plain clothes detectives. He glanced at Beth and she found herself averting her eyes. Embarrassed. Guilty.

She should have done something. Looked for Debra earlier.

'We could go out again,' she told her parents. 'Join the search. That's where Tonya's gone, I think.'

Beth wondered what had happened to Miriam. She'd seen Miriam's dad arrive, tense and stressed. Heard Miriam giving a statement, which hadn't amounted to much because Miriam couldn't remember most of the evening. And then, at some point in the blur of time which followed, Miriam had gone.

Clutching her mother's arm for support, Beth managed to stand up. Outside, the sound of distant sirens and a few dog handlers with German Shepherds searching the immediate area of the pub. If Debs had passed out somewhere, as Beth had, at first, feared, they'd have surely found her by now. But, if not that, then what? Phone calls had been made to all her friends. Local houses were being checked to see if she'd staggered to one of them. So far, nothing.

As they stood, wondering what to do, a lady officer approached. One of the ones who'd interviewed Beth earlier.

'We're doing our best, love,' she said, as Beth started to cry again. 'We'll find her. You ought to go home now. Get some sleep.'

'I want to help,' said Beth firmly.

In the end they drove round in their car. Following the route to Tonya's. Back to the pub again. To Debra's and back. Through the town centre. Along some of the back roads. Being stopped twice by police checking traffic. All the time listening to the local radio broadcasting news flashes about Debs. If the police hadn't taken it seriously at first, they certainly were now. The first couple of hours were crucial, one of the cops had said, if someone had been abducted.

Debs hadn't been, Beth told herself. She hadn't! The phone would surely ring soon. But it didn't and the minutes and hours ticked by until they finally went home, exhausted. Beth's parents insisted she lay down. Tried to get some sleep. As if!

She closed her eyes though, while her mum sat beside her stroking her hair. Half dreaming, half awake, Beth was back in the pub, watching Debra, seeing where she went, who she spoke to, what she did. And suddenly Beth knew what was wrong with her statement.

Fiona Cardew sat staring at the coffee the police officer had made her. Her husband was staring out of the window, as he'd done since returning home, while Lori lay on the settee, crying.

'I'm sorry,' one of the police officers said, 'to go over it all again but we need to cover every possibility. Is there anywhere else you can think of where Debra might have gone?'

Fiona shook her head, pain searing down her back as she did so, stomach tightening sickness welling in her throat.

'Is there any reason she might have run away? Was she under any stress? Were there any problems at home?'

'No,' she said. 'I've told you. We hadn't argued. There weren't any problems. Debra was fine. And before you ask again she wasn't into internet chat rooms. We'd have known! She wouldn't have gone off with anyone. Not Debra.'

'She didn't always tell you everything,' said the police officer gently. 'You didn't know she was at the pub, did you?'

'She told *me*,' said Lori, looking up. 'Even if she didn't tell Mum and Dad things, she'd tell me.'

'So you'd know if she was using drugs?'

'Drugs!' screamed Lori. 'Debra! She doesn't even smoke. Barely drinks!'

'That's what I'm getting at,' said the officer. 'Friends told us that Debra seemed very drunk at one point. But then one of them, Beth, phoned us about half an hour ago, wanting to change her original statement. She said she hadn't really thought about it at the time but she's sure now that Debra hadn't drunk *that* much. She hadn't finished her wine at Tonya's house and had left a couple of drinks at the pub virtually untouched. So not really enough to make her ill, or make her act out of character, Beth thinks.'

'So you reckon Debs took something?' said Lori. 'No way! No way at all!'

'All right,' said another officer, trying a different tack. 'We're working our way through everyone who was in the pub or at that party. But it's going to be a long job. So I'd like you to look at the list we've put together so far. Tell me if there was anyone Debra was particularly close to. Anyone she might have had a reason for leaving with. Or anyone who might have had an interest in Debra.'

Fiona Cardew scanned her copy of the list.

'There's dozens of people Debra knew,' she said. 'All her friends.'

She paused, looked at Lori, knowing she'd focused on the same name.

'I think we should tell them,' Fiona said.

'It's nothing,' said Lori, looking over at the police officers and then at her dad.

But her dad wasn't listening. He'd found something of his own, swung round and punched his fist into the wall.

'Three teachers!' he yelled. 'On that list! Three teachers watching a pack of under-aged kids get drunk. Well they won't have jobs to go to next term. I'll bloody make sure of that.'

'All right,' said a police officer, grabbing Robert Cardew's arm. 'All right. Calmly now.'

'Calm!' he yelled. 'My daughter's missing and you tell me to be calm!'

But he allowed himself to be steered to a chair, while another officer nodded at Fiona to go on.

'Lori's been getting threatening letters and text messages,' Fiona said.

'What?' said Robert Cardew, leaping up again.

'And have you reported it?' asked the officer.

'No,' said Lori, her voice shrill. 'There was no need. No point. I knew who they were from. It's Stefan, my ex. He's an eejit but he doesn't mean anything.'

The policeman who was sitting at the table with a laptop suddenly looked up.

'We've got two or three statements saying that Debra had some sort of argument with this Stefan.'

'So?' said Lori. 'It would have been about me! He's always pestering her about me but he wouldn't hurt her or anything. He wouldn't hurt anyone.'

'How do you know?' her dad said. 'How do you know what that drug-crazed lunatic might do? Why didn't you tell me? Why didn't you tell me about the letters?'

'Because he was threatening to harm himself!' Lori said, her voice suddenly uncertain. 'Not me. And not Debs. Not Debs!'

'Maybe,' said the officer. 'But I think we need to have a word with him. Now!'

Chapter 5

Against all expectations, Beth had finally slept but by ten o'clock she was back at the pub with dozens of others who'd volunteered to search or be interviewed.

'It's awful,' said Amy Parker, coming up and hugging Beth. 'I can't believe it. I mean I know me and Debs didn't always get on but—'

'Yeah, right,' said Beth, pushing her away.

'You don't think she's run away or anything?' Amy said. 'Because of—'

'You?' said Beth. 'No, I don't. I don't think it had anything to do with you. So I hope that makes you feel better, Amy. I really do. Because sorting out your guilt hang-ups is like *really* high on my list of priorities at the moment.'

Beth stormed off. Sniping at Amy was pointless. She knew that. But right at this moment she wanted to hit out at anybody and everybody. Just to relieve the tension. To give her something to do. The trouble was, it didn't work. She'd been snapping and shouting at Mum from the minute she woke and all it had done was make her feel worse. Tightening the pain across her ribs so she could barely breathe.

'Hey,' a voice behind her said.

Beth turned to see Benny. Cuddly Benny who held her close, letting her sob onto his chest, soaking his tee

53

shirt, until a police officer rounded them up and sorted them into groups. Beth wiped her eyes, tried to concentrate as a cop told them where they were going, what they had to look for, how they were going to work. Their group was assigned to an industrial complex further down the road. Owners had been called in to open up their premises. But it wasn't inside that they were likely to find anything. It was outside. Places where things might have been dumped. Clothes or...

Beth couldn't even think about it. Couldn't even say the words in her own head. Instead she forced herself to believe that any minute now Debs would appear or the phone would ring and everything would be OK. Or she'd wake up. It would be Saturday morning. Not Sunday. The whole thing one crazy, paranoid nightmare. If only.

The group was strangely quiet. Even Benny, who normally couldn't keep his mouth shut for more than thirty seconds, had still only said that one word, 'Hey'. Everyone was concentrating on the search. Desperate for clues, however small. And that's the way it stayed for an hour or more until the buzz went round that the police had arrested someone. Beth wasn't sure which of the rumours were true or how they started but by the end of the day, the area round the pub was alive with them.

'It's Stefan,' Miriam said. 'They've arrested that ex-boyfriend of Lori's.'

'They haven't arrested him,' said her cousin, Eddie. 'They've been talking to him. That's all. Like they've been talking to everyone.'

54

'Yeah, but I heard they're doing him for possession,' said Omar.

'And harassment or something,' said Safira. 'They raided that grotty flat where he lives and took away his computer and cannabis plants but they can't think he's got anything to do with...you know...or they'd have held him, wouldn't they?'

'They do that though, don't they?' said Miriam. 'Sometimes. If they haven't got enough evidence. If they want to trick someone. They let them go, don't they? Then watch them.'

'Bitch!'

The word lodged in Beth's head, blotting out the real conversation going on around her. Echoing over and over. And with the word came an image of Stefan's face. The look in his eyes when Debra had refused to take the note. A look of desperation. But how desperate?

'Just 'cos he's supposed to be a druggie and have a thing about Lori,' Benny was pointing out quietly, 'doesn't mean he'd *do* anything, does it?'

It was strange, Beth thought. The way they all avoided saying Debra's name. And that the only certainty, the one thing they knew for sure, was the one thing that nobody mentioned outright. The fact that Debra was still missing.

They've questioned me. Well, they were bound to, weren't they? I expected it. It's nothing to worry about, is it? They're questioning everybody. People who were in the pub. People who drove past the pub. People who live near the pub. Neighbours. Friends.

Sort of scary but it gave me a bit of a buzz too. Going over what I saw, what I heard, who I spoke to, what I said, where I'd been, where I went. Most of it was true which made it easier. You should never lie when you don't have to. Keep the lies for when you really need them. That way they're easy to keep track of, aren't they?

And when the police started asking about my connections with the family, I just admitted it, didn't I? Sure we've had our differences but that doesn't mean I'd wish them any harm, does it? Wouldn't wish this on anyone. You'd have to be a real sicko, wouldn't you, I told them. To want anyone to go through this.

Worst bit was when they started going on about other stuff. Stuff that had nothing to do with Debra going missing at all. I nearly lost it then. But I managed to get a grip. Forced myself to keep calm. They weren't really interested in all that, I reckoned. The problems I've had. They were just trying to rattle me. They do that, don't they? Try and get you off guard. So I changed the subject. Went back to Debra. Kept saying how awful it was. How I couldn't concentrate for thinking what might have happened to her.

I even distracted the police with a couple of ideas of my own. Mentioned the name of someone. They nodded like they'd already thought about him. Maybe even interviewed him already. But I'm not sure the police are really thinking local at all. Rumour has it they're trying to tie it in with a few other missing persons cases. Some going back a couple of years. Well that's just fine by me. Let them keep busy with their databases while I plan my next move. Because it's not over. Oh no. I've barely begun.

★

56

The last group to return to the pub was the group that had been searching along the disused railway track. Beth could tell by their weariness that there'd been nothing. Mr Mason nodded at her and Tim Simmonds seemed to look right through her before slouching off to his car. Marc left his family and came over to her and Tonya.

'They're doing an appeal,' he said, almost to himself. 'On the news tonight. Debra's parents.'

'Yeah, I know,' said Beth, staring at Marc.

He was white. Absolutely white. Even his eyes seemed to have drained of colour.

'I . . . it's . . .' he said, looking around nervously. 'The cops asked to interview me again this morning. They came round to the house. I mean, are they doing that with everyone? Second interviews?'

Beth sighed. She might have known. That this was more about him than Debra. Or was she being mean?

'Not everyone,' said Beth. 'Some people.'

'They've been round to our place twice,' said Tonya. 'Kept on about Mum covering up where we went. Like we might be hiding Debs or something. Helping her to run away! It's crazy! Mum's in a right state. She felt guilty enough as it was.'

Marc looked round again, staring at his brother.

'What is it?' said Beth.

'Nothing. It doesn't matter.'

'Marc!' said Beth, grabbing his arm, letting her nails sink in. 'What are you on about? If you know something, *anything* that might help.'

'I don't,' said Marc. 'It's nothing like that. Honest. I'd do anything, tell them anything, if I thought it would help. But it won't.'

There were tears in his eyes now. Macho, motor-mouth Marc was standing in front of her sobbing and she didn't know what to do. Even worse, Beth thought as she walked away, she didn't care. If Marc hadn't been such a bastard then maybe Debs would have been with him at the end of the night, instead of . . . where? Where was she? Was it already too late?

Watching the TV appeal later, Beth even found herself getting angry with Debra's parents. They were reading a statement. Begging Debra to come home. Telling her that whatever she'd done, it would all be all right. If only she'd get in touch. As if Debra was hiding out somewhere, winding everybody up. For a laugh!

'They have to do that,' Beth's mum told her. 'They have to cover every possibility. Even if they know Debra wouldn't have run away. They have to try.'

The appeal had moved on. Asking for witnesses. Pleading for people to come forward. But there'd been hundreds already. Beth knew that. The police were ploughing through statements, watching hours of CCTV footage from all over town, following leads that led nowhere. And with every second that ticked away, the chances of finding Debra grew fainter.

'Please God,' Beth said aloud. 'Please don't let her be dead. Please don't let her be dead.'

She'd never prayed before. Not ever. She'd mouthed

the words in assemblies but they'd never meant anything. Now they meant everything.

It was dark. Totally dark. Except for a funny, tiny star of blue light floating around inside her head. Behind her eyes. Turning red. Then white. Then disappearing altogether. Her eyes were open, she was sure. But something was pressing on them, as though someone had blindfolded her. Hurting. Her eyes were hurting. She couldn't see. Couldn't see anything. Or hear anything. But she wasn't alone. She was sure she wasn't alone. Someone was there. Watching her. She could feel them, sense them.

She tried to shout out but she couldn't. Her mouth was sore. Dry lips forced apart, tongue aching. Something was there. In her mouth. Stopping her from crying out. Couldn't move either. Arms, legs, paralysed or tied down? She could turn her head but it hurt so she stopped trying.

Where was she? She could feel movement, as though she was in a car. But there wasn't any noise. So was this a ghost movement? A memory of a journey? Like the other memories, jumbled in her head. Laughing. Shouting. People talking. Talking to her.

'Debs.'

She was Debs. Debra.

Debra. Debra. Debra, she told herself over and over. Trying to hold on, as the voices faded, as the blankness came again. And the room, that wasn't even there, spinning around and around and around. Churning sickness. Mustn't be sick. Mustn't let it happen. Mum would come soon. Turn the light on. Help her.

Someone was here, now. She could feel them coming closer. Had they been there all the time? Watching her? Who? Not Mum. Wrong smell. Nice smell, though. Someone nice. Pulling the thing from her mouth. Trickling water on her lips, down her throat. Cold. Ice cold. Funny. Silly. Not scary. So thirsty. So very thirsty. Don't take it away. Not yet. Listen to me. How can you? I'm not talking. Can't talk. Only in my head. Lips won't move. Nothing works. Nothing works. I want to go home. Don't do that. Please don't do that. I need to sleep. Get up. Go home. Why won't you take me home? Don't do that. No! Don't leave me. Don't leave me here. I want my mum. Help me. Why won't you help me?

'You've got to help us. If anybody knows anything, you've got to help us.'

Lori's voice, pleading, desperate, echoed in the room long after Beth had turned the TV off. The image of Debra's face was imprinted on Beth's eyes. The video clip they'd used for the appeal wasn't one Beth had seen before.

It was Debra, in their garden dragging a piece of string which their cat, Kipper, was chasing. As Kipper leapt on the string, Debra looked up straight into the camera. Smiling. Looking as though she was going to walk right out of the TV set. Then the camera zooming in close. On the dark hair flopping round her face. On the eyes. Blue. Bright blue. So alive.

And people all over the country would be talking about her. Such a pretty girl. Clever too. Just passed all those exams...such a shame. Writing her off! As though she was already...

'I feel so helpless,' Beth's mother was saying. 'I want to phone but, well, they probably don't want anybody. Will they?'

'We're not just anybody,' said Beth. 'We're their friends, for heaven's sake. Probably their closest friends. I mean what if everybody thinks like you're doing? What if everyone's too worried, too embarrassed to do anything? They might want someone, mightn't they? Someone to talk to?'

'Beth's right,' said her step-dad. 'I mean, we ought to, I don't know, at least offer some help. Even if they don't take it.'

'Not tonight,' said her mother. 'There might be calls following the appeal. I'll phone in the morning. First thing in the morning. I promise.'

In the end it was Beth who phoned. On Monday morning. Just after Mum had announced she was taking the day off work because no way did she want Beth to be on her own.

There wasn't any news. Not really. There'd been plenty of information following the broadcast but nothing concrete as yet. Nothing helpful. But yes, Mrs Cardew had said. It was all right to come round.

As soon as Fiona Cardew put the phone down it rang again. This was how it had been all morning. Family, friends, well-wishers. Starting with Beth an hour or so ago. The police had offered to take the calls but Fiona had insisted on doing it herself. Talking was better than thinking. Doing something rather than nothing. Keeping busy.

Detective Sergeant Avery nodded at her to pick up and continued listening in. Monitoring, recording everything, just in case.

'Hello, Fiona Cardew.'

'It's Alice,' the voice said.

Fiona shook her head. Alice? Who on earth was Alice?

'Alice Hall,' the voice explained.

'Oh,' said Fiona.

Dr Hall's wife. Surely the woman must have heard? Surely she didn't want to talk about her husband right now?

'I won't keep you,' she said. 'I just wanted to say how sorry I am. And I hope she's all right. I really am sorry. I hope you find her.'

The phone clicked off. But before Fiona could even begin to imagine why Mrs Hall, of all people, should have phoned, it rang again.

'Hello, Fiona Car...'

'I saw your appeal,' a voice interrupted.

Northern accent. Distorted. Fake. Like someone with a heavy cold. Someone trying to disguise their voice.

'I know where she is,' said the voice, as Fiona's hand began to shake.

'Who *is* this?' said Robert Cardew, snatching the phone, while Lori grabbed hold of her mother to stop her falling. 'Who are you? Where's Debra?'

Fiona saw Avery frantically signalling at her husband to keep talking. As they'd been primed to do if they got a call like this.

'Where is she?' Robert yelled. 'Where's Debra? Just tell me. What do you want? We'll do anything!'

'Look in the school.'

Then a snort like suppressed laughter before the phone went dead.

Robert slammed it down. Picked it up. Dialled 1471. 'Withheld number.'

'It's all right,' Fiona heard Avery say in the middle of a barrage of orders and the frantic burst of activity that exploded around her. 'We're on to it. We'll get a trace. Get a team out to the school.'

'I'm going too,' said Mr Cardew, heading for the door.

'All right,' said their family liaison officer. 'Wait a minute, while we organize a car. But don't . . . don't get your hopes up. It's probably a hoax. You'd be surprised how many nutters there are out there. People who think it's funny. Attention seekers.'

'OK. We're getting a fix on the phone,' Avery said. 'Mobile.'

Fiona clutched onto Lori. Automatically tried to move towards the front door as she heard it open. Got no more than two steps before a uniformed officer walked in, telling them the car was ready.

'Mum?' said Lori.

Fiona nodded.

'I'll be OK,' she said. 'Go with your dad. If you want to.'

Shortly after they left, Beth and her mother arrived. Fiona barely had time to tell them about the call when news came through that they'd traced the owner of the mobile.

'No,' said Beth, the name thudding in her head, over and over. 'It can't be. That can't be right.'

Chapter 6

Beth sat between Tonya and Benny on the low wall outside Miriam's house. Safira was leaning against the 'Sold' sign. Omar stood with a small group of lads, heads down, hands in pockets. Miriam was with her parents and Eddie, in the garden, on the other side of the wall.

Somehow everyone had congregated at Miriam's. Probably because it was near the school. Their school, where the police had spent all day searching and found nothing. The call had been, as suspected, nothing more than a sick hoax.

'I can't believe it,' Tonya was saying, as people had been doing all day. 'I just can't believe a teacher would do something like that. Make a hoax call!'

Beth stared at her, trying to focus, trying to hear the words. But she was so exhausted, so totally drained, that the simplest things seemed impossibly difficult. Even breathing. Several times, she'd felt on the verge of passing out. Had to remind herself to take deep breaths.

'He didn't!' Omar was saying. 'You know he didn't. It wasn't him. Mr Khan didn't even have his mobile. He'd lost it!'

'That's what he's saying now,' said Beth wearily. 'That's what he's telling the police. But he didn't tell anyone at the time, did he? He didn't report it missing.'

'Well you wouldn't, would you?' said Omar. 'The

police don't do nothing about missing phones! Maybe he thought he'd just left it in the pub or summat. Then with Debs going missing. Well, he forgot, didn't he?'

All the lads were defending Mr Khan. He was one of the popular teachers. Like Mr Mason. One who'd always have a laugh with you. So would his idea of a laugh be a hoax call? Part of Beth thought not but, on the other hand, what else could you believe? His story just didn't seem true.

'Forgot!' she muttered. 'Sure.'

'It's possible,' said Eddie.

'How do you know?' Beth said, more sharply than she'd intended. 'You don't even know him!'

'No,' said Eddie. 'But what I mean is, I've lost my mobile too. I was sure I had it in my pocket on Saturday night. Then when I came to use it on Sunday, it wasn't there. And I didn't tell anyone either. I mean, you don't, do you? You think it'll turn up. But what I'm saying is, if they both went missing from the same place, I mean, has anyone else lost a mobile?'

He looked around as everyone shook their heads.

'So you reckon,' said Beth, 'that someone might have gone round nicking mobiles just so they could make hoax calls? Before anyone even knew Debs was missing? It doesn't make sense, does it?'

Eddie flushed, hung his head, looked embarrassed.

'I don't know,' said Miriam's dad. 'Eddie might have something. It's worth a mention. I take it you haven't told the police yet, Eddie?'

'No,' he said. 'Not yet. But I will. If you think it's important. I'll do it now. Can I use your phone?'

Beth watched Eddie slouch inside and felt guilty for being mean to him. He'd got enough troubles of his own, with his dad in prison, yet he was still trying to help. He'd been out searching. Because Debs was Miriam's friend, maybe? Or just because. There'd been plenty of people out there, offering support, who didn't know Debs or the family.

One or two that you wouldn't have expected at all. The mad 'bag lady' who hung around the precinct, had somehow found out and come to help. A group of builders had downed tools and joined in. There were mums with babies in pushchairs. Debra's granddad who'd recently had an operation and shouldn't be out at all. He was there searching with a dozen of his friends from the golf club. And a lad called Simon from the lower sixth.

'I was dancing with her,' he'd told Beth. 'With Debra. Then she just walked off. I thought she'd dumped me so I went home. But I shouldn't have done, should I? I should have gone after her, then maybe . . .'

Maybe. If only. The words Beth had used so often herself. But it didn't help. Nothing helped. Even with half the town involved, they hadn't found anything. Anything that would help get Debra back.

'The thing is,' Safira was saying, 'you can't really trust anybody, can you? Even teachers. I mean Mr Khan and his phone, Mr Mason and his dodgy alibi.'

'What do you mean?' said Tonya.

'His alibi,' said Safira as though it was common knowledge. 'When the cops first talked to him, he made out as if he'd left the pub with the other teachers, didn't he? But he didn't. He left earlier. On his own.'

'How do you know?' said Benny. 'How do you know all that?'

'Ryan told me,' said Safira. 'His next door neighbour's a cop, isn't he? So he might have got it from him.'

He might have done, thought Beth but, on the other hand, Ryan might have made it up. There were so many rumours going round.

'Yeah well, it's not hard to guess what Mr Mason's covering up, is it?' said Omar.

He raised his eyebrows as everyone turned to look at him.

'Mrs Craig?' Omar said. 'You must have heard? I reckon he might have sneaked off to meet her or summat. I mean he wouldn't want to say about that, would he? With her husband being an ex-army bloke.'

'Mrs Craig! The school secretary?' shrieked Safira. 'Mr Mason and Mrs Craig? You must be joking. She's twice his age! And we know he likes 'em young!'

Beth shook her head. How could they do this? Stand there chatting, spreading school gossip as if this was an ordinary day? As if Debra was with them. Laughing. Joining in.

'Good job I phoned,' said Eddie, coming out of the house. 'The police said a couple of other people reckon their phones were stolen. On Saturday night. At the pub.

That's at least four. I mean, it might be coincidence, of course.'

It had to be, Beth thought. Because if it wasn't . . . then whatever had happened to Debs had been planned. Premeditated. By someone who knew her. But who? Who would do that?

There was one person. One person Beth had mentioned in her statement. Then felt guilty about it. But looking back on it now, there was definitely something a bit odd, a bit over-familiar in the way he'd spoken to Debs at the school. Then turning up at the pub like that. As if he was waiting for her. Beth wondered whether the police had followed it up. Whether they'd spoken to Tim Simmonds yet.

It was sort of funny seeing it all in the paper. Took up most of the first four pages. Knocked that plumber bloke's porn trial right back to page five. Which was silly really because they didn't have much to say about the Debra business. It was mostly background stuff. About her life, her family, her friends. Wonder how the Cardews feel about that? Having their own lives picked over, for a change!

Paper mentioned the search of the school but didn't go into details. Rattled on about how upset Debra's friends are. How they've been offered counselling.

Counselling. People seem to think it's the answer to every-thing these days, don't they? Talk to a bloody counsellor and it will all be all right. But it didn't help me and it won't help them either. Or Debra. Once I let her go. If I let her go.

Oh, I know I meant to. Meant to let her go after a few hours, I think. Sunday evening. Once the panic had time to set it. But I didn't. Couldn't, could I? Not with police swarming everywhere, prying into everything. I didn't realize how big it was all going to get so quickly. It's amazing how fast the police move when it's a family like the Cardews!

But it doesn't matter. I've made it safe enough. In my special hiding place. Debra hasn't seen me. Hasn't heard me speak. Doesn't know where she is. I mean, I'm sneaking back whenever I can. Keeping her so drugged up she doesn't even know what planet she's on, I reckon.

That's the problem, though, isn't it? Give her too much and she'll OD. Or puke up. What if it happens when I'm not there? She'd choke herself, wouldn't she? With that gag in her mouth? But I can't risk removing the gag or blindfold. And if I ease up on the dose she might start to notice something. Something important. But then, it doesn't really matter, does it? She won't remember, will she? I don't know. Haven't thought it all through. Haven't had time. Not with everything that's been going on. I'm having to make most of it up as I go along.

Not just because of all the activity either. There's something else. I didn't know when I started all this how it was going to get to me. How much I was going to enjoy it. Playing with them. All of them. Answering their questions. Pretending to be upset, shocked. Pretending to care. Sending them off on false leads. Getting them to do whatever I want.

I've got so many ideas. Dozens of them. New ones springing into my head all the time, while Debra's lying there. Totally helpless. Waiting for me to decide. Me! My decision. Except it's

70

getting a bit tempting, is that. Knowing I could do anything.
Anything I wanted. Ask for ransom money. Take pictures. Send
them to her parents. Pictures in lurid poses. Or maybe I could
arrange her with her eyes closed and arms folded over her chest.
Like she was dead. Yes, pictures are a good idea. I could do that
now, couldn't I?

Whatever I do, Debra won't argue. Not that I'm going to
touch her or anything. Not like that. I know they call it the Date
Rape drug but that's not what I'm about, is it? I'm thinking
what I can do to them. The family. All the games I could play.

But no. I should bring it to an end. I really should. The longer
I keep her, the more chance I have of being caught. Making a
mistake. Doing something I don't really want to do. So, OK, I
need to think of something really dramatic, don't I? Something
I can do before I let Debra go. Something that will really screw
them all up. Twist the knife one more time.

It was funny. It was dark. Totally dark. But she could see
herself. Lying on some sort of bed. As though she was
looking down at herself. And the girl on the bed was
sobbing, choking. But the one in the air was happy, free,
floating. Two different girls? Or the same one? Had she
split herself in two? It didn't matter. It was nicer this way.
Because she didn't want to be back down there. With the
one on the bed. All dirty, stained, sweaty, smelly. It was
scary down there. It hurt. That's why she'd escaped. Up
here there was no pain. It was like bouncing on
marshmallow. Soft, squidgy, warm, cosy. Nothing could
hurt her up here.

71

Maybe if she tried really hard she could float right out through the ceiling. If there was a ceiling. Right up to the clouds. Following the light. The tunnel of light that was drawing her up, holding her, fixed in its beam. Bright, like angels. And below her now, a garden. Two girls. Small. Shrieking. Running. Playing.

'You can't catch me, Beth! You can't catch me! I'm flying, Beth. You'll never catch me now. I'm up here. Up here, Beth. Look at me.'

Only one girl now. Looking up.

'Debra, come down. Come back. You can't go. I won't let you go. Debra!'

Not floating now. Someone slapping her face. Shouting her name. Pulling her, hitting her. Can't see. Can't see. Can't talk. Only in my head. Don't do that. Stop it. You're hurting me. Don't want it. Won't drink it. Don't want to. Please don't make me. Want Mum. Want Dad. Want to go home. Why won't you listen? Nice smell again. That smell. Like herbs or... Who are you? Let me go. Let me go. You're hurting me.

What are you doing? Want Mum. And Dad. And Debra. No not Debra. I'm Debra. Silly. Want to float again. You can't touch me up here. Won't come down. Won't let you hurt me. Want to play with Beth again. Can't catch me! I'm flying. I'm flying. No, stop that. Stop it. Leave me alone! I can't breathe. I can't breathe.

Fiona Cardew stared at the clock on the shelf. Almost midnight. Not that it mattered. Time wasn't working

72

properly anymore. It had stretched somehow. Dragging itself out agonizingly slowly. Taunting them. Like the lunatics who kept phoning the incident room. Their liaison officer said it always happened. Every time they appealed for help with a crime, there'd be hundreds of genuine calls but, scattered amongst them, the hoaxers, the nutters, the attention seekers.

Was Mr Khan one of them?

Robert didn't think so. He was angry with him for being at the party. Thought he'd been unethical and irresponsible. But he wasn't malicious, Robert had said. Not the sort to make a hoax call. The police agreed. The school call, they thought, was different from the others. It could well have been made by the abductor. On Mr Khan's stolen phone.

The police were having the voice analysed. They'd been able to trace roughly where the call was made from. But none of it was helping. Nothing was happening! They hadn't found her. Might never find her.

Fiona heard a scream. Realized it was coming from herself. Bringing people running. Lori. Robert. A WPC. But they couldn't help. She was beyond their reach. Drawing in on herself. She could barely hear them. Their voices a blur of background noise. Then another noise. The phone ringing. Pulling her back. Her hand reaching out instinctively to snatch the receiver.

'Hello... hello? Who is this? Hello?'

Silence.

'Hello?' she said again.

73

No answer.

She was about to slam the phone down when someone spoke.

'It's time,' the voice said. 'Time to say goodbye. Say goodbye to Debra, Mrs Cardew.'

The same voice. The same phoney northern drawl.

'No...please...stop this...stop this...'

Breathe, Fiona. Must breathe. Keep breathing. Keep calm. Keep him talking.

'It's your last chance, Mrs Cardew. You want to talk to her, don't you? You'd like to say goodbye?'

Don't scream. Don't make her panic. Keep calm.

'Debra! Debra? Can you hear me?'

'She can't answer you. But yes, she can hear you. The last voice she'll ever hear. Now say goodbye.'

No. Not that. Not that. Say something. Say something to her.

'We love you, Debs. We love you so much...'

The sudden click freezing the room. An explosion of noise inside her head, outside her head. Words. Screaming anger, love, despair, hope, disbelief, desperation.

Then the silence.

The darkness descending.

Beth got out of bed, moved towards the window. She didn't know what had woken her. But there was something. Someone. Out there. In the garden. She got up, pulled back the curtains, looked down onto the lawn. It was light. Amazingly light. She could see the

74

figure quite clearly. Standing by the tree. Looking up at her.

'Oh my God, Debra!' she screamed. 'Debra!'

What was she doing there? Out in the garden. Looking up, smiling, waving, as if nothing was wrong. As if it wasn't the middle of the night at all. As if she'd never been missing. Where had she been? What was she doing? What was going on?

'Debra,' she screamed again. 'Wait, I'm coming down.'

Beth swung round, headed for the door but it wouldn't open. Someone had locked it. Someone had locked her in!

'Mum! Let me out. Let me out. It's Debra. She's outside.'

Hands gripping her shoulder. Someone hugging her.

'Let me go!'

'It's OK, it's OK,' her dad said, squeezing her tighter. 'You were dreaming.'

'No,' said Beth, pushing him away. 'She's there. Outside. I saw her!'

Beth paused. Not her room. She wasn't in her bed-room. She wasn't even in her own house. She was in Dad's house. In the lounge. At the front. So she couldn't have seen the garden. Not from there. And besides, it wasn't his garden she'd seen. It wasn't even her own garden at Mum's. It was Debra's.

'I don't understand,' she said, shaking her head. 'I saw her. I really saw her. But I couldn't have. It was *her* garden I was seeing. Debra's garden.'

'Like on the TV appeal,' said her dad. 'That's what you were remembering, that's what you saw. In your dream.'

All the excitement, the euphoria, disintegrated in an instant, leaving Beth drained, exhausted, shivering, crying.

'You fell asleep,' said her dad. 'On the settee. I didn't like to wake you. Even when you started to cry out.'

'It was Debra,' said Beth, desperate to cling on, desperate to believe.

'I'm sorry, love,' her dad was saying.

'I know,' Beth said. 'Don't keep saying it! I know!'

It wasn't real. Couldn't have been real. She knew that now. But it was almost real. Too strong, too vivid, for a dream. But if not a dream?

She was shaking her head again. Trying to push it away. The feeling. The knowledge. The certainty. But it wouldn't go. It wouldn't let go.

'It's over!' she screamed out. 'What I saw. It was Debra. And she's . . .'

'Stop it! Stop it, Beth,' said her dad, holding her close again. 'It was a nightmare, love, that's all. Not a premonition. Nothing sinister. Ssshh, now. You saw Debra because you wanted to see her. It doesn't mean anything. Come on, go to bed now.'

'I want to go home,' Beth sobbed. 'I want Mum.'

'I'll take you back,' said her dad. 'First thing in the morning.'

'Now,' said Beth. 'I want to go home now. I don't care what you say. Something's happened. I know it has. I have to go home!'

Chapter 7

It's all gone wrong. I didn't mean to do it. Not like that. She forced me into it. Debra. I tried to give her more stuff. But she didn't want it. Started thrashing around, spitting it out. And I hit her. Not hard. So it couldn't have been that. The slap couldn't have hurt her. It was just to get her attention. Make her drink. And she did. In the end.

She settled down. She seemed OK. I only left her for a few minutes. To make the call. Because I couldn't get a signal in there. Didn't want Debra to hear anyway. I was only pretending that bit. To wind them up. It was all pretend. I didn't mean it. I didn't mean any of it. But then . . .

It had all changed. When I got back. I couldn't wake her. I couldn't. No matter how much I shook her. It was awful. When I pulled off the gag, her tongue was blue and swollen. And behind the blindfold, her eyes were solid. Lifeless. Like false eyes. Lumps of glass. And cold. She was so cold. She had blankets. I'd given her blankets. Looked after her.

They won't believe it was an accident. Not now. Because I'd already made the phone call. Making out I was going to kill her. But I wasn't. I was only trying to scare them. I'm not a murderer. I'm not like that. I'm not a murderer. It was Debra's fault. Debra spoilt it all. She wouldn't wake up. She wouldn't come back. I decided to get rid of her. Quickly. Get her away from there. Not sure I should have done that. But it's too late now. And besides, it will be all right.

It was dark. No one saw me carry her out. I'm sure they didn't. They couldn't have. But I'm worried about the cameras. CCTV. Speed cameras. They've got them everywhere, haven't they? Spying. Watching every move you make. And I had to drive her a fair distance, didn't I? Before I dumped her? Somewhere quiet. Somewhere no one would see.

I was careful, though. Really careful. Didn't panic. Not even when she groaned. It terrified me, that. Because I thought she was dead. I honestly thought she was already dead. But she wasn't. And I didn't know what to do. I wanted to help her but I couldn't. So I cut the ropes round her hands and feet with a camping knife and just left her.

Drove home. Cleaned up. Hid the ropes and all my clothes. Ready to burn or bury when I get a chance. Because they can pick up the slightest thing these days, can't they? Maybe there's evidence all over Debra. But they won't be able to pin it down, will they? Because all sorts of people must have touched her that night. Everyone was hugging and kissing. Brushing past each other. And I was careful. Wore gloves all the time.

They'll find her. Someone's sure to find her soon. In the morning, maybe. I hope so. Because I didn't mean it to end this way. Maybe I should go back. Pretend I found her. By accident. Play the hero. No. Too risky. But if she dies? That might be better. Safer. Might have happened already. But I don't want that. Never wanted that. It's not my fault. Calm down. Think it out.

Phone call. One more phone call. That's all it takes. Tell them where she is. Do it now. Before it's too late.

★

Beth was slumped in the passenger seat of the car. The radio was on and her dad was talking but she didn't hear any of it. It had been a mistake to go to Dad's. She hadn't wanted to. Hadn't really wanted to do anything. But Mum had said it was best. To try to carry on as normal, as much as possible. Normal! How could anything be normal anymore? But she'd been too tired to argue so it had all been arranged.

Dad had picked her up from Miriam's. Taken her for a pizza, which she hadn't been able to eat. Tried to tempt her with ice-cream. As if she was a kid again. As if ice-cream could solve her problems. Bring Debra back. Make it all better.

Then, when they got back to the house, he'd presented her with a laptop, as a present for passing her exams. His wife, Shelley, had bought her a couple of CDs and the kids had made her a card. Beth had tried to look pleased, or at least interested, but it hadn't worked. The results, which they thought so brilliant, didn't seem to matter any more. What was the point of being clever if you couldn't even look out for your best friend? Shelley had shrugged, Dad had looked hurt, as Beth had rushed from the room in tears.

It wasn't really Dad's fault that he couldn't help. She loved him and she was sure he loved her. He was trying his best. Trying to distract her. But he didn't understand. Not in the way Mum did. At least he'd agreed to take her home. They were nearly home now. Just passing the half-built supermarket. Maybe it would be best to give Mum a ring. Warn her they were about to turn up.

As Beth got her mobile out she heard something. Sirens. Getting closer.

Her dad slowed down as first an ambulance, then a police car raced past on the other side.

'Turn round, Dad,' Beth said, as she looked out of the rear window to see the emergency vehicles swinging into the supermarket site. 'Turn round!'

'Why?' her dad said.

'Debra,' said Beth. 'It's something to do with Debra. I know it is.'

'I doubt it,' said her dad, driving on. 'It could be anything. Vandals. Drunks.'

'Turn round,' Beth shouted, as another police car passed them.

'This is crazy,' her dad sighed, preparing to turn.

'No it isn't,' yelled Beth. 'Didn't you see? Didn't you see who was in that police car?'

Was it a hoax? Another hoax? The building site, the second call had said. The supermarket site. Be quick, the voice had said. As if there was still hope.

They had been quick. They were heading there now. Teams with searchlights had been called in. Paramedics. Just in case.

The radio was crackling and the officer in the passenger seat talking. Fiona tried to make out what he was saying but it was as though someone had put a black hood over her face, drawn it tight, blocking all her senses. And when she did finally hear, she could barely believe it.

'They've found something,' the officer said, turning round.

'Something?' Robert snapped. 'What kind of something? What do you mean?'

'Someone,' the policeman said. 'They think it might be...'

The radio started chattering again, halting his words as the car turned into the supermarket site.

'It's her!' the policeman announced.

'Are you sure?' Lori screamed.

'They're sure,' the policeman said.

'Is she...?' Fiona began.

'She's alive. In a bad way but she's alive,' the officer confirmed.

Impossible. Almost impossible to believe. Alive. They'd found Debra. Alive.

'How bad?' Robert was shouting, leaning over, reaching into the front of the car. 'Can I talk to her? Let me speak to them.'

Everything seemed to be happening at once. Robert talking, Lori crying, the car screeching to a halt. Somebody helped Fiona out of the car. A police officer she thought, though it might have been Robert. The glare of blue lights flashing momentarily blinded her as she hurried forward. Then the glare of headlights, as another car raced towards them, coming to a sudden halt.

Beth got out. Beth, Fiona thought. What was Beth doing there? With the police, the paramedics, the vehicles, all in a hopeless jumble of movement and noise.

'Where is she?' Fiona shouted, as someone steered her round the back of an ambulance. 'Where's Debra? Let me see her.'

Her eyes rested on a stretcher being hurried towards the ambulance doors. She saw the grey blanket, black straps, oxygen mask, tubes everywhere, the blood pouring from Debra's face.

'Oh my God!' Fiona whispered, before her legs gave way.

It hurt. Everything hurt. Someone had told her it was all right. But it wasn't.

'Debra? Debs, can you hear me?'

Debra opened her eyes but the bright light forced them shut again.

'Debra?'

Don't do that. Stop that. I want Mum. Why won't you listen? No words. Words still won't come out. Mouth won't work. Feel so sick and hot. Far too hot. Got to get out. Outside. Where it's cool. What are you doing? Don't want that. So tired. Just want to sleep. Can't sleep. Something crawling on my face. Make it go. Make it go away.

'Debra? Debra, leave that, love. Try to leave it. It's oxygen.'

Hands touching hers. Not nice. Push them away. Pull the thing off her face. It wasn't nice. She didn't want it there.

'Debra, it's me. It's all right, love. It's me. You're safe.'

'Mum?'

Mouth working now. Heard that. Can talk. Can't see though. Can't open eyes. Too bright. Hurts.

'It's all right, Debs, I'm here. Nothing's going to hurt you now. You're in hospital.'

Silly. Not Mum. Dream. Sounds like Mum. Still talking. Try to listen.

'You're in hospital, Debra.'

'Hospital? How long?'

'It's Wednesday,' her mother's voice said. 'They brought you in yesterday. I've been with you all the time. We've been talking. Do you remember?'

Debra shook her head. Groaned as the pain shot through her shoulders, down her back.

'I've been playing,' she said.

'Playing?'

'In the garden. With Beth.'

'And do you remember anything else?' her mother asked. 'About where you've been?'

'Floating,' said Debra. 'I've been floating and playing. It's too bright. I can't see. I want to see you. So I know you're real.'

'Try again,' said her mum. 'I've turned the light off and closed the blinds. See if you can open your eyes.'

Debra opened them, slowly. She saw the tube sticking out of her hand, saw her mother's face, pale and anxious. Tried to remember.

'An accident?' she said. 'I've had an accident?'

'Sort of,' said her mother.

'Where's Dad? Where's Lori?'

'They'll be here soon. They'll both be back soon. You remember them?'

Funny question. Why shouldn't she remember? She nodded.

'Good,' said Mum, as though she'd done something brilliant, something amazing.

Like passing her exams. They'd been pleased about that. She'd been pleased. They'd gone to that Italian restaurant where the crazy waiter kept flirting with her and Lori. Gave them giant ice-cream sundaes. On the house, he'd said.

'When did it happen?' she asked. 'The accident?'

'After the party,' her mum said. 'Do you remember the party?'

'Sort of,' said Debra as a few images filtered into her brain.

Amy yelling. Miriam's manic laughter. Benny sliding around on his knees.

'And do you remember leaving?' asked her mum.

'Dancing,' said Debra. 'I was dancing. I don't remember anything else. Did something happen at the pub? I wasn't supposed to be there! I was supposed to be at Tonya's! I'm sorry. I'm sorry.'

'It doesn't matter,' said her mum. 'It doesn't matter where you were. You're safe now.'

'But what about Beth and Tonya and...'

'They're fine. It was just you, Debra. You—'

'What?' said Debra. 'What happened to me?'

'We don't know,' said Mum. 'We're not sure. You disappeared, Debra. From the party.'

Debra heard herself giggle, though she didn't quite

84

know why. It sounded funny somehow. Disappearing.

'You went missing,' her mum was saying. 'Sometime after midnight on Saturday. We found you in the early hours of Tuesday morning. Unconscious. On a building site.'

Midnight on Saturday. Tuesday morning. Debra tried to count up the hours but her brain wouldn't work. It was a lot. A lot of time. Where had she been? Building site? She didn't remember a building site.

'Why can't I remember?' she found herself saying aloud. 'I can remember other stuff. Why can't I remember where I've been?'

'The doctors have been doing some tests,' Fiona said.

She paused. Looked at her daughter. Made a decision. She would tell Debra herself. She wouldn't wait for the doctor or the counsellor.

'They've found traces of drugs in your system, love.'

'Drugs?' said Debra. 'No way! That's not true. I don't do that stuff. You know I don't. Ask Beth, ask Tonya, ask anyone!'

'It's all right,' said Fiona, clutching Debra's hand. 'No one thinks you *did* anything deliberately. It seems that someone might have slipped something into your drink.'

'My drink?' said Debra. 'You mean like...so they could...'

Was that why she couldn't remember? Because someone had spiked her drink? Like those cases they'd looked at in school? In PHSE? Date rape cases!

'Nothing happened,' said her mother urgently. 'Not

85

like that. The doctors would know if anything had happened. And it hasn't.'

'You mean they've been touching me?' said Debra, shuddering. 'Examining me?'

'They have to,' said her mother.

'And I didn't know?' said Debra.

'You were awake,' said her mother. 'You were conscious. I was with you.'

'But I don't remember. I don't remember coming here. I don't remember what they did. I don't remember what happened before. Anything could have happened. Anything! And I wouldn't know! I *don't* know!'

Her voice was rising, shrill, hysterical. Her head was crashing onto the pillow. Over and over. Trying to shake something loose. Trying to remember. Floating again. Looking down at the girl. The other girl. The one that wasn't really her. The one that couldn't be her. The one things had happened to. Things she didn't even *want* to remember.

Chapter 8

Beth stood outside Debra's house, on Saturday morning, not wanting to ring the bell but knowing she must. Wondering what she'd find when she went inside. They'd let Debs out of hospital yesterday afternoon. They'd said she might make more progress if she was home. Beth hoped they were right but, from what Lori had said on the phone, it didn't sound hopeful.

The newspaper reports, the TV coverage had all been so jubilant when Debs had been found. With good cause, in a way. In most cases like this, it all ended so very differently. So very much worse. The media had wanted Beth to do interviews but Mum hadn't let her and Beth was glad. She didn't want to. Didn't want to describe what it had been like seeing Debs lying there on that stretcher. Face pale and bruised. Blood gushing from her nose. Groaning. Whimpering.

Images that Beth would never forget, never be free of. But, even having witnessed it first hand, Beth had been naive enough to think, for a while, that it was over. Debra was back. She'd get better. Life would move on. They'd get back to normal.

Now, of course, she knew differently. Which was why it was taking her so long to ring the bell. She'd been to the hospital three times a day, every day. Sometimes Debs would see her, sometimes not. And Beth was never sure which was worse.

Slowly she raised her hand, let it hover over the bell but before she could press it, the door opened.

She's home now. She's OK. She's safe. But they won't let it drop. The police are everywhere. Still snooping round, asking questions. Even ran a special news report. The abductor was highly dangerous, they said. Would almost certainly strike again! Why do they do that? Winding everyone up, with their stupid theories, spreading panic.

They got in a so-called expert, who rattled off a psychological profile of the kidnapper. Probably a loner. An obsessive. Possibly someone who collects things. Someone who likes to be in control.

Well no one's going to recognize me from that, are they? It's nothing like me, is it? I don't collect things. Apart from my pictures and that's not what you'd call a collection, is it? And I'm definitely not a loner. I like my own company sometimes but so do lots of people. It doesn't mean you're a loner, does it? As for the control . . . well, I've never been in control of anything at all, have I?

I mean, they don't know anything, do they? They don't know anything about me. They've picked up on the fact that I'm probably local. Known to the family. Harbouring some sort of grudge. Well, I gave them enough clues, didn't I? But not enough to pin anything down because there are dozens of people who hate the Cardews. All the people she's nailed in her paper for a start and most of his pupils, probably.

They haven't said anything about Debra. Whether she's remembered anything. Told them anything. But she can't have done. She can't have seen me. Not even when I took the blindfold off. Not the way she was. She couldn't have seen anything.

Trouble is, they do all that forensic stuff these days, don't they? Trace someone from a single fibre sometimes. Which is why I've burnt everything now. The blankets, the gloves I wore. The shoes. Her shoe. Everything.

So I reckon I'm safe. Keep my head down for a bit. Be careful what I say. They're bound to let it drop eventually, aren't they? It's not like she's dead or anything, is it? I didn't hurt her. They've got her back. What more do they want?

'She's in the shower again,' Lori said, as Beth followed her into the kitchen. 'Can I get you anything? Coffee?'

Beth nodded, staring out of the kitchen window at the long garden she'd seen in her dream. This time it wasn't Debra she saw, it was Mr Cardew, working his way along the neat flowerbeds with a hoe.

'It doesn't need doing,' Lori said, following the direction of Beth's gaze. 'We have a guy comes round twice a week.'

'I know,' said Beth.

'Dad doesn't even like gardening,' said Lori, starting to cry. 'He's just doing it because—'

She grabbed a piece of kitchen towel, wiped her eyes, blew her nose.

'He'll probably kill everything Stan's been growing for us these last few years,' said Lori, forcing a laugh. 'But that's not the worst thing.'

The laugh faded.

'That's not the worst thing Stan's had to put up with,' Lori said. 'The police have been questioning him. Checking his house, his allotment. He's 72, for heaven's sake. He wasn't even near the pub that night, as far as we know. But they're checking everyone. Everyone who's ever had anything to do with us.'

She looked up as she heard the sound of a door opening upstairs. Feet padding across the landing. Turning. Retracing their steps. Door closing again. The sound of plumbing, water gushing.

'She does this,' Lori said. 'Just like she did in the hospital. Comes out of the shower, then goes straight back in again. And when she's not showering she's bathing. When she's not bathing, she's washing. Nothing we say, nothing the doctor or the trauma counsellor says, makes any difference.'

'It's early days yet,' said Beth, knowing how feeble, how inadequate, it sounded.

'Yeah, that's what Mum keeps telling me but—'

'Where is she?' said Beth, thinking it strange that Mrs Cardew wasn't around.

'She's popped into work for a couple of hours,' said Lori. 'She's still signed off but she's gone to pick up some stuff she might be able to do from home. You know, something to take her mind off things. And she's got a meeting with someone. That photographer. Tim Simmonds. Another one the police won't leave alone.'

'Yeah, well,' said Beth. 'I'm not surprised. In his case.'

Lori shook her head.

'You don't know him,' she said. 'I mean, I don't, really. Not that well. Not as well as Debs. But he's always struck me as a bit of a softie really. Not the sort to harm anyone. Even with the drinking, he doesn't get violent or anything. He's a nice bloke.'

Maybe too nice, Beth thought. What if his 'niceness' was the wrong sort. The perverted sort. Lori was naive and far too trusting. Too eager to think the best of everyone. Even now, when you couldn't trust anyone. Didn't Lori know that the nicest people could change under the influence of drugs or drink? That everyone was open to temptation, to pressure. You only had to look at Councillor Wilcox and the way he got so hooked on the very worst kind of porn. But there was no point saying anything. It was a miracle Lori had any faith left in human nature at all, after what had happened, so why spoil it?

'Is it OK if I go up?' she asked. 'Give Debs a shout?'

''Course,' said Lori. 'Try to get her to come down if you can. She hasn't had any breakfast or anything yet. I don't know what's going to happen when term starts. I'm thinking of taking a year out of Uni so I can look after her. I mean that would be easier, wouldn't it, than Mum or Dad giving up work? Dad's still talking about getting Debs back to school but he's kidding himself. There's no way. No way at all. She won't even see anyone outside the family... you're the only one.'

And not even me, most of the time, Beth thought, as she stood outside the bathroom.

'Debs,' she said. 'It's me. Beth. Are you coming down?'

'I'm in the bath.'

'I know. I mean, will you be down soon?'

'Yeah, soon,' answered Debra, though without any conviction.

Beth wasn't even sure she wanted her to come down. It was hard to know what to talk about. So impossible to know what to say.

'Just talk about normal things,' Mrs Cardew had urged the previous morning, at the hospital. 'Friends and stuff.'

So Beth had talked about friends. For half an hour or more. But Debra hadn't listened. She'd been somewhere else. *Someone* else almost. Face impassive. Eyes dull.

'She just wants to know,' Mrs Cardew had said as Beth was leaving, 'what happened to her and why. But we can't tell her. The police can't tell her. Because we don't know. And we're not getting any nearer to finding out. Might never find out.'

Lori's mobile was ringing when Beth got to the kitchen, so she hung back, not wanting to pry but Lori signalled her in.

'Look,' Lori was saying. 'You're not supposed to be phoning me! Yes, I know you're worried. And well, she's just the same. Yes I will. I know, Stefan! No, of course not. And thanks for the flowers.'

'Flowers?' said Beth as Lori ended the call. 'He sent you flowers?'

'No, not me,' said Lori. 'Debra! He's really cut up about it all.'

'I bet!'

The words were out of her mouth before Beth could stop them.

'I know he's an eejit,' said Lori. 'I think even Stefan knows it. But—'

'He wouldn't hurt anybody, right?' said Beth. 'But somebody did, didn't they? Somebody hurt Debs.'

'Yes,' said Lori. 'But not Stefan and not Tim. Even the cops don't think Stefan could have done it. They want me to press charges, though,' she added, 'about the other stuff. The text messages.'

'But you're not going to?'

Lori shook her head.

'Too many people have been hurt already,' she said quietly. 'Why add another to the list? What good would it do?'

Lori was right. Hurling anger around, lashing out at everyone and everything wouldn't help. But how could Lori be so sure about people? That was what Beth couldn't understand.

'Besides,' said Lori, as she opened the door to let Beth out, 'I'd rather the cops spent their time trying to find the kidnapper rather than harassing Stefan over the drugs or poor Marc about his brother's car. Because until they do, there's not a chance of Debs getting better. And I can't stand it. I can't stand watching her like this.'

She clung onto Beth, sobbing, until Mrs Cardew drove up and took her inside. Beth looked up at the bathroom window as she left and thought she saw the curtain move but when she looked again it was totally still.

★

Debra drew back from the window. She'd wanted to wave to Beth, shout to her to come back but she hadn't. Because she couldn't be sure who else was out there. Watching. Waiting. If he wasn't there now, he would be. Eventually. She knew he would. He'd come back. Whatever the police said, whatever her counsellor told her, she knew she was right. Whoever it was would want to know. Would have to check. Maybe they already had. Maybe they'd already been to the house. Bringing flowers or chocolates. Offering sympathy. Which is why she wouldn't see anyone. In case it was him. Or someone who'd been in contact with him. Touched him.

She moved quickly to the sink, started to wash her hands, stared into the mirror. Really deep inside it. Trying, as she did all the time, to see into herself. Reach the memories. They must be there. There must *be* something. Some hint, some clue about the missing days.

'Say goodbye. Say goodbye to Debra.'

She'd listened to the tapes. Knew them off by heart. Tried to hear something in the voice, the messages. Something familiar. Some way to identify the bastard.

What had he done to her? Why hadn't he carried out his threat? Why hadn't he killed her? Had she fought him? Resisted him? There were no signs of a struggle, the police had said. No traces of anyone's blood or hair under her nails. No evidence that she'd scratched or bitten. So what had she done? Sat there, stood there, lay there while he did whatever he wanted? But how could she have fought? Drugged up like that? Not even knowing what

94

was happening? But she should have done. It was no excuse. She should have done something. Should remember something. It was her own fault. All her own stupid fault.

Her eyes switched from the mirror over the sink, to the mirrored doors of the bathroom cabinet. But it didn't matter where she looked, how she looked, they wouldn't come back. The memories wouldn't come back. Only the dirt. The dirt kept coming back. On her skin. Under her skin. Dark little bubbles, oily stains, spreading like bruises no matter how much she washed them away. She could feel them now, crawling beneath the surface, ready to burst out. Stop them. Have to stop them.

Her hand reached out, opening the cabinet door. Just as she'd done last night. Feeling along the bottom shelf until she found what she was looking for.

How could Lori be so sure? The question wouldn't leave Beth. How could Lori trust people like Stefan and Tim when Beth found it impossible to trust anyone at all?

Even now, walking home along a busy street in broad daylight, she found herself looking round. Hurrying on each time a car slowed down, keeping a distance every time someone walked past. Suspicious of everyone.

Suspicious of the people who phoned asking about Debs. And there were dozens every day. Beth had become their natural link to Debra but were all their motives genuine? Or was one of them sick, psychotic, gloating? Marc? Simon? Simon seemed incredibly interested for someone who'd only danced with Debra once. She'd even caught him hovering near to Debra's house one day. Said he'd been to drop off a card, which turned out to be true. So was she being paranoid? Yes, totally, was the answer. But it wasn't something she could stop, something she could control.

On Thursday afternoon she'd even refused a lift from Mr Mason. She and Tonya had been to the hospital, knowing that Debs probably wouldn't see them but going anyway to leave a card signed by all her friends. Mr Mason had been on a similar errand. Taking a card and present from the staff.

He walked with them down three flights of stairs, talking all the time. But more sort of professional, more distant than before. Then outside, seeing it was pouring down, he'd offered them a lift. Tonya had been all set to follow but Beth had grabbed her sleeve, babbling about Mum coming to pick them up.

'It's all right,' Mr Mason had said. 'I understand. I shouldn't have offered.'

'I don't,' Tonya had said, as he strode off. 'I don't understand. He's a teacher, Beth! He'll have had a million police checks. There's two of us! What did you think he was going to do?'

Beth didn't know. But she wasn't prepared to take any chances. Not with anyone. Not while the abductor was still on the loose.

Chapter 9

'Miriam phoned, while you were in the bath,' Fiona
Cardew said. 'She's having some friends round tomorrow
night. Just a few. Before she leaves. She wondered
whether you'd...'

Debra shook her head.

'I could go with you,' Lori said. 'Just for half an hour,
maybe.'

'No!' Debra screamed, as she rushed out of the room.
'Leave me alone! Leave me alone!'

'I'll talk to her,' Robert Cardew said, touching his
wife's arm as she prepared to stand. 'Make your mum a
cup of tea, eh, Lori?'

'How did it go this morning?' Lori asked as she filled
the kettle, talking all the time to blot out the sound of
Debra's crying. 'Did you get any work done? How did
you get on with Tim?'

'I've brought work home,' said Fiona. 'I don't really
have to. They're all doing fine without me. I'm obviously
not as indispensable as I thought. But I was glad I went.
Just to get away for a bit. I'm sorry. That sounds awful,
doesn't it?'

'No,' said Lori, handing over the tea. 'No, it doesn't.'

'And Tim...well, Tim was the best I've seen him for
ages. A bit uptight, with the police going back to him
time and time again but he swears he hasn't had a drink

97

since the night Debs went missing. I'm not sure I believe him. I've heard it all before. But I didn't push it. Not sure the meeting did any good in that sense at all. He just wanted to talk about Debs all the time.'

'What did you tell him?'

'What I tell everyone,' she said. 'All the psychobabble the counsellor spouts at us. That it's going to take time. Patience. Time and more bloody time. But I don't believe any of it. That's the trouble. When I told Tim what she was like, how contaminated she feels, how she washes her hands all the time, scrubbing them till they bleed, he cried. We both cried. But no amount of tears is going to do any good because when I look at her, Lori, I don't see Debs anymore. And I don't think I'm ever going to get her back.'

'We will,' Lori said. 'She's going to get through this. She's going to get better, Mum. She has to.'

It wasn't much of a party, Beth thought. But then, how could it be? With the packing cases stacked against the walls, a grim reminder that, by this time next week, Miriam would be gone. They'd all be back at school or college. Everyone except Debra.

'I'm not sure I even want to go anymore,' Miriam had said. 'I mean it hasn't been too bad recently. No hate mail or midnight phone calls when the line goes dead. And I'm beginning to think Mum's right. It feels too much like running away. Giving in. As though it's us that's guilty.'

In the pause that followed Beth had wanted to say

something, offer sympathy or reassurance but couldn't find the words.

'Part of me thinks,' Miriam went on, 'that we should stick around, give Uncle Gordon some support. Go and see him, like Mum does. But then, when I think about what he did...all those pictures...of little girls...it makes me feel sick and I know I don't want him near me...looking at me! Dad's even worse. Says he'd probably kill him if he saw him. Then Mum gets all upset and they start shouting at each other and—'

Miriam had paused again, looked, for a moment, as though she really was going to be sick and still Beth couldn't find the words of support she wanted to say. It was almost as though she had no emotions, no feelings left. As though they'd all been crushed out of her, leaving her lost and silent. With no sympathy left to give.

'But it's not only Uncle Gordon we're walking away from now, is it?'

'What do you mean?' Beth had asked, snapped from her lethargy by this sudden shift in the conversation.

'It's Debra as well. I know she doesn't want to see anyone right now but she's going to need her friends, isn't she? Eventually. And I won't be there, will I? I won't be able to help. I can hide from my problems but she can't hide from hers, can she?'

'We'll keep in touch,' Beth had said, hugging her. 'Even if you can't tell us where you're going, you can phone, can't you? You can phone Debs. When she's better. It's not the end of everything.'

It wasn't the end of everything, Beth thought later, as she perched on a packing case, sipping a glass of water. It just felt like it. She turned as the lounge door opened and Benny came in, followed by Marc and Amy Parker.

Why her? Beth wondered. Why had Miriam invited Amy? It was only supposed to be a few close friends and Amy was hardly that. The look on Miriam's face, as she came through from the kitchen carrying a tray of pizza, told Beth that Amy hadn't been invited. She'd just tagged along with Marc. Not that it really mattered. Debs wouldn't care who Marc was with. She didn't care about anything anymore. Not ordinary things like friends or boys or music or make-up.

'Hi,' Marc said, disengaging Amy from his arm and heading straight for Beth.

He kept his head down as he spoke, didn't look at her directly but Beth noticed his right eye was bruised.

'How is she?' he muttered. 'How's Debs?'

Beth told him as much as she could, as much as she knew.

'It's not like you think,' Marc said quietly, glancing over at Amy.

'I don't think anything,' said Beth. 'It's none of my business, is it?'

'What I mean is,' said Marc. 'I care about Debs ... you know...'

'But not quite as much as you care about yourself,' Beth said, sliding down off the packing case.

'Don't be like that, Beth,' said Marc, grabbing her arm. 'I told the police everything in the end. Even about the

100

argument over the car keys. About driving. Even though I knew I'd get done for it.'

'What a bloody hero,' said Beth.

'It kicked off another massive row with our Dean,' he said. 'That's how I got the black eye. Then Dad thumped Dean and Dean's moved out and—'

'Like I care, Marc!' said Beth, pulling away and marching into the kitchen.

As she stormed through the door, she crashed into someone, spilling the remains of her water down a grey shirt.

'Sorry,' she said.

'S'all right,' Eddie mumbled. 'I'll get you another. What do you want?'

'Water. Just water, thanks.'

There were only three people in the kitchen. Eddie, Miriam's mum, who was rather viciously cutting up a chocolate cake, and Miriam's dad, who was grabbing things out of cupboards and packing them in boxes. Clearly this room was off party limits. Apart from all the packing, the atmosphere felt tense, aggressive. As though there'd been an argument, which was about to break out again, any minute. Miriam's dad kept glancing at her mum, who ignored him and stared, instead, at Eddie as he poured the water. As if she didn't really want him there at all.

Beth half-smiled at Miriam's parents, said hello, took the glass of water from Eddie.

'I'm just giving them a hand,' he said, as though he felt it necessary to explain his presence.

He smiled. The same slightly embarrassed smile he'd had on the night of that other party. No wonder the atmosphere was tense! If it was bad for Miriam, with her parents constantly arguing about Gordon, thought Beth, as she drifted back into the lounge, what must it be like for Eddie? Right at the centre of it. And then there was that other business, which must surely have upset him. About the phone.

'You OK?' Miriam asked. 'You look miles away.'

'I was just thinking about Eddie.'

'Eddie?' said Miriam, a little edgily.

'His phone. It's a good job he reported it missing when he did or he'd have been dragged through all the questioning, wouldn't he? Like poor Mr Khan.'

'Eddie's phone was used for the really nasty call, wasn't it?' said Benny as he and Marc came over to join them. 'The "Say Goodbye" call. The one they played on TV.'

'Yeah,' said Miriam. 'Then the abductor used another stolen phone to make the last call. About the super-market site.'

'But they still can't track him,' said Marc. 'I mean, whoever it is, he's not stupid, is he? It was all really well planned, clever—'

'Sick,' said a voice in the doorway.

Everyone turned to see Eddie, glaring at Marc.

'Not clever,' Eddie snarled, without a trace of his usual shyness or embarrassment. 'Sick. Totally sick. They should bring back the death penalty for people like that.'

Not so long ago, Beth thought, she'd have been horrified by a statement like that. Would have leapt in to argue. But now, thinking about Debs, how she was when they found her, everything she was going through, Beth wasn't so sure. It seemed no one else was either. There was silence for a moment. Total silence, until Marc suddenly spoke.

'No,' he said. 'The death penalty's never right. Even for serial killers and stuff. And specially not for people who are sick, as you put it. 'Cos if they're sick, then maybe they can't help it.'

Beth stared at him, amazed. Liberal and reasoned argument wasn't quite what she'd expect to be coming out of Marc's mouth. Especially under the circumstances. When it was so personal. When almost everyone in the room would have probably killed Debra's abductor themselves, given half a chance.

'I know it's Debs we're talking about,' said Marc, looking around, sensing opinion was against him. 'But however bad someone is, however sick, you can't just kill them off. I mean, we're not even talking about a murderer here! He let her go, didn't he? Even told the cops where to find her. Maybe he was sorry. He could have killed her but he didn't!'

'He will though, won't he?' said Eddie. 'He'll kill someone, one day, if he isn't stopped. Even if they find him, even if they put him away, he'll be out after five years or so, won't he? Then maybe some other girl won't be so lucky.'

'Eddie's right,' said Miriam, as one or two people, including Amy, nodded their support.

'Fine,' Marc snapped, pointing at Eddie. 'Great. So does his "string 'em up" philosophy apply to other cases? Other sickos? Porno-addicts and paedophiles perhaps?'

Beth heard one or two people gasp. Eyes were flickering between Marc and Eddie. She saw Benny move forward a couple of paces, ready to stand between them. Expecting a fight. Saw tears streaming down Miriam's face.

'My dad looked at pictures,' Eddie said. 'A few bloody pictures. Because they were there. Because they were available. Because they were pushed at him. He didn't touch anybody, he didn't harm anybody, he didn't wreck anyone's life. Except maybe his own. And mine. And you think that's the same, do you? The same as someone who drugs and abducts a girl?'

Eddie's anger-fuelled confidence suddenly collapsed.

'I'm sorry,' he muttered, backing out of the room. 'I'm going.'

Miriam's quiet tears gave way to loud sobs. Several people tried to comfort her but she pushed them away.

'Miriam,' Marc said.

'Leave it, Marc,' Amy said. 'Just leave it.'

'Miriam,' he went on. 'I'm sorry. I didn't mean . . . you know I didn't . . .'

'Get out!' she screamed. 'All of you. Get out!'

Everybody's still talking about it. You can't go anywhere without someone mentioning Debra, or the family or the abductor. And it's not helping. It's really not helping.

To be honest, all I want to do is forget about it. Get on with life, like it never happened. But I can't, can I? I shouldn't have done it. I know that now. I don't know why I did it. Why I went through with it. It was like, once I'd thought about it, I just couldn't stop myself.

Trouble is, I'm still thinking about it. And it's sort of confusing. Because in one way I'm glad it's over but in another way. . . No, forget that. I've done what I wanted to do. Got my revenge. The family are in pieces. Just like I wanted them to be. Only it's not as good as I thought and I'm not sure why. Maybe because they don't know. They don't know it was me, do they? They don't know what they're paying for or why I made them suffer. And I can hardly tell them, can I?

So the job feels unfinished, somehow. And that's dangerous, isn't it? Dangerous for me. Because I keep wanting to do something. Something else. I can feel the idea, like a hard, little seed, lodged in my brain. And I know it's going to burst open, sending roots and shoots scurrying everywhere. Growing, feeding, taking over, so in the end I won't have any choice. Because it's been like that with everything recently. Like I don't have any control at all. I just do things. And it's not me. It's not really me.

I've been round there a couple of times. Didn't go in. The policeman on duty outside said the family didn't really want to see anyone. It wasn't a risk, being seen there, talking to the cop, like that, because loads of people have done the same. Friends, well-wishers, the curious.

People pretend to be shocked, pretend to care but they lap it all up, don't they? The drama, the sleaze. That's why the tabloids and the reality shows on telly do so well. People just can't get enough of it.

So why disappoint them? It's not as though I'm going to get caught. They're all so thick. They haven't got a clue, have they? And my new plan's nothing like as risky as the original one. Why even think about it? Why bother to fight it? I'm going to do it. I know I am.

Chapter 10

Fiona opened the door to show the counsellor out. It was strange not seeing a policeman standing there. But it had been their own decision. To dispense with the close protection. To try to get back to normal. And they'd stuck by their decision. Even after what had happened last night.

'I thought she wasn't too bad today,' the counsellor said, smiling.

Fiona nodded, though she didn't agree.

'We talked through this new problem, then I tried to end on a more positive note,' the counsellor said. 'Get her thinking about the future. She seemed quite interested in the idea of starting her sixth form work from home, then building up slowly. Going into school one morning a week.'

Saying it and doing it, Fiona thought, as she closed the door, were, unfortunately, two completely different things. It was Monday today, sixth form induction day tomorrow, with term starting properly on Wednesday. And there was no way Debs was ready for that. No way at all. She wasn't even able to concentrate on anything, let alone summon the courage to go back into school. Especially after this latest setback.

Fiona fixed a smile on her face as she prepared to go back into the lounge. It was important to stay cheerful and positive around Debs, the counsellor had said. But it wasn't easy.

'It's nothing!' Debra was screaming at Lori, as Fiona opened the door. 'I told you, Kipper did it. When I was playing with him this morning.'

'What is it?' Fiona asked. 'What's wrong?'

'Nothing!' Debra yelled, pointing at Lori. 'It's her! Making out like I'm some sort of nutter. Saying I'm cutting myself or something.'

'I didn't,' Lori said. 'I noticed some scratches on Debra's arm, that's all.'

'Oh yeah,' said Debra. 'And then you wouldn't believe it was the cat!'

'All I said,' Lori protested, 'was that Kipper never uses his claws.'

'Can I have a look?' Fiona asked. 'At the scratches?'

'No!' said Debra, as she stormed from the room. 'No you can't.'

'They weren't cat scratches, Mum,' said Lori, starting to cry. 'What are we going to do? If she's hurting herself?'

'We don't know that yet,' her mother said. 'Not for sure.'

'I do!' said Lori, as they heard the sound of water running. 'I know what I saw. At first I thought it might have been a reaction to what happened last night but some of the marks didn't look recent. They looked like they were healing. So she could have been doing it for days, couldn't she? Cutting herself! Even at the hospital?'

'I don't know,' said Fiona. 'We'd have noticed, wouldn't we? But it's possible. The way Debs feels about herself, anything's possible. I mean that's what the counsellor's supposed to be sorting out. Trying to get Debs over this crazy idea that it was, in some way, her own fault! But I'm not sure Debs really opens up with her. In fact I know she doesn't. She tells the counsellor what she wants to hear. I mean—'

The sound of the doorbell stopped her.

'I'll go,' said Fiona. 'It'll be Omar's mum. She's picking up some shopping for me. I didn't really need her to. She insisted! Everybody's been so good.'

But it wasn't Omar's mother with the shopping. It was someone else. Someone who Fiona hadn't expected to see.

'She wouldn't see me this morning,' Beth told Tonya. 'And even Lori didn't want to talk much. They'd had another phone call. Late last night.'

'What do you mean?' Tonya's mother said. 'What kind of phone call?'

'They think it was from the kidnapper,' Beth said. 'Not a mobile. From a pay phone this time. Same voice though.'

'Saying what?' asked Tonya. 'Why would he phone now? Now Debra's back?'

'I'm not sure,' said Beth quietly. 'But he says he's got photos. Awful photos. Says he's going to post them on the net.'

'Oh my God,' said Tonya.

'It might not be true,' said Tonya's mum. 'He might just be saying that.'

'Or maybe,' said Tonya, 'the call wasn't from the abductor at all.'

'It's possible,' said Beth. 'That was the risk of playing it

109

on TV. That some other nutter might pick up on it. Copy the accent. But the police don't think so. They wanted to keep a guard on the house but Debra's mum wouldn't have it.'

'I'm not sure that's wise,' said Tonya's mother. 'If it was me, I'd want someone there 24/7.'

'They're still watching,' said Beth. 'From a distance. I passed a cop car myself. On the corner of Debs's road. And Lori says they've got teams checking the net, waiting for something to appear.'

'Does Debra know?' said Tonya. 'About the call? About what he said?'

Beth nodded.

'She was there when he phoned. Flipped completely, Lori said. Just stood there, screaming. And she wouldn't let anyone hold her or hug her or even get near. She won't let anyone touch these days. Not even her mum.'

'And can't they do anything?' Tonya said, helplessly. 'The doctors, the counsellor?'

'It seems to be getting worse, not better,' said Beth. 'And I think the only thing that's really going to help is if they catch him, lock him up. Even then, I don't know if it'll be enough.'

'I keep thinking,' said Tonya, 'about that phone call. That other phone call. "Say Goodbye." I mean, it's true, isn't it? It's not really Debra that's come back. The Debra we knew.'

Beth shook her head. Tonya was right. And if he was going to keep making phone calls, keep torturing her, putting terrible photos on the net, she wasn't ever going to get well, was she?

'Why can't they find him?' she said out loud. 'It must be someone who was around that night. Someone we all know. I can think of loads of people who had the opportunity. Even a motive. But no one who's that psychotic. No one!'

Fiona stared at the woman on the doorstep.

'Yes?' Fiona said.

'I need to talk to you. I phoned your office. They said you weren't there.'

'No,' said Fiona. 'I haven't been back. Not properly. It's my deputy you need to see. He's dealing with everything.'

'It's not about my husband,' Alice Hall said. 'Not really. Can I come in?'

Fiona was about to refuse but Mrs Hall had already pushed past her.

'Mum?' said Lori, opening the lounge door. 'What's going on?'

Fiona shrugged as Mrs Hall marched into the lounge and turned to face them.

'I had to come,' she said. 'I've been following it all. In the papers. On TV. I even helped look for her.'

'Thank you,' said Fiona. 'But I don't see—'

'It's all connected,' said Mrs Hall, pacing up and down, as she'd done that day in the office. 'And nobody's doing anything about it.'

Fiona looked at her, bewildered. Mrs Hall's face was

burning. Her hair was wild and frizzy, as if she hadn't combed it for days.

'What happened to my husband,' Mrs Hall said. 'What happened to Debra. It's connected. We're living in a sick society, Mrs Cardew. Completely sick.'

'Look,' said Lori. 'I'm sorry but Mum doesn't need any of this right now.'

'You don't understand,' said Mrs Hall. 'I'm trying to help. Trying to explain. We're obsessed. Completely obsessed. It's everywhere. Everywhere.'

'What is?' said Lori.

'Sex!' Mrs Hall shouted. 'Pornography! In the newspapers, on TV, on the internet. You can't get away from it. That's how James got caught up. He wanted to stop it. Do something about it. But he couldn't. It corrupted him. Changed him.'

'I'm sorry,' said Fiona. 'I really am but—'

'Then they go out, don't they?' Mrs Hall went on. 'These teenage girls. Children. In their crop tops and short skirts and make-up.'

'Hang on?' said Lori. 'What are you saying? That it was Debra's fault she was abducted? That she's some sort of tart? That we shouldn't be allowed to dress up on a night out?'

'No!' said Mrs Hall. 'But we're sending out all the wrong messages, aren't we? Look, drool, leer. . . is it surprising that some men take it too far? Is it surprising that they can't stop themselves? Even in your own paper, Mrs Cardew, it's all sex, sex, sex.'

'My paper!' said Fiona. 'It's a local evening! A family paper. We don't have anything like that!'

'Look,' said Mrs Hall, pulling a few pages of roughly torn newspaper out of her bag and dumping them on the table.

'That's an art exhibition,' said Fiona, looking at the first one. 'We were reporting on an art exhibition. Photographing paintings. And even then, Tim shot them from a distance so they wouldn't look too graphic.'

'Nudes!' Mrs Hall snapped. 'They're still nudes whatever distance you photograph them from. Do you think nice, decent, ordinary families want to open their evening paper and see those staring out at them?'

Lori tried to catch her mother's eye. This woman was unhinged. Seriously unhinged. Lori took her mobile out of her pocket. It was time to put a stop to it but her mother shook her head.

Mrs Hall shuffled the papers.

'And that!' she said.

Fiona and Lori looked at the picture of the woman in the black lacy bra and pants.

'It's an advert,' Fiona pointed out. 'For lingerie. Perfectly harmless and reasonable. And even if it wasn't, I can't censor adverts.'

'No,' said Mrs Hall. 'Nobody censors anything anymore, do they? That's the trouble. Look at the internet. Pop-ups advertising porn sites, e-mails about penis enlargements, sites devoted to cannibalism and suicide. The very worst kinds of perversions. Feeding the sickest imaginings.

113

Fantasies, which can break out, become real. Look at that German cannibal. And the man who kept a dead woman's body in a shed. They both fed their fantasies on the net, didn't they? They admitted it. Were proud of it, even!'

Lori was still poised with her mobile. Mrs Hall had lost it completely. Wringing her hands, shouting out example after example. But Fiona still wasn't sure she wanted Lori to phone the police. Part of her felt sorry for Mrs Hall. Part of her even believed she might have a point or two, in amongst all the rambling. Not about her paper, of course, but maybe about the tabloids and the net.

'And this,' Mrs Hall was saying, pushing another piece of paper towards them.

Fiona looked with tears in her eyes. There was nothing sleazy or even mildly distasteful about this one. It was just kids cheering, celebrating their GCSE results. Tonya, Beth, Omar and, right at the front, Debra. The happy, lively Debra who barely existed anymore.

'Look at them,' Mrs Hall snapped. 'Half-dressed. Bra straps showing. Skirts up to their behinds.'

'This is ridiculous,' said Lori. 'You can't possibly think a picture like that has anything to do with the sort of stuff you've been talking about. The sort of thing your husband's been looking at. *Chose* to look at. And that's what you're trying to do, isn't it? Blame Mum. Blame Mum's paper. Blame the internet. Or society. Find excuses for him. Because this is all about him, isn't it? Your pervert of a husband. It's got nothing to do with Debra. You don't care what happened to her at all.'

114

'I do care,' said Mrs Hall. 'I'm just trying to make you understand how someone, someone quite ordinary, might see these things and get messages. The wrong messages.'

She paused and they all turned, hearing a slight sound, a gasp. They saw Debra standing in the open doorway, swaying, staring, eyes wide for a moment before she collapsed.

Lori and her mother darted forward, knelt by Debra, hardly looked at Mrs Hall as she edged past.

'I'm sorry,' she was muttering. 'I didn't mean...I didn't think...I just wanted to...I'm sorry. I'm so sorry. I'll go now. Yes, I'll go. I must. I'm sorry.'

'Phone the doctor,' Fiona told Lori, as they heard the door slam behind Mrs Hall. 'And go and get your dad. Debra? Debra, are you OK?'

Debra groaned as she started to come round. She pushed her mother away. Lay, for a while, totally still.

'She didn't mean anything,' Fiona said, unsure of how much Debra had heard. 'She wasn't blaming you. It was nothing to do with the way you were dressed or what you did. It wasn't your fault, Debra. Nothing about it was your fault.'

'That smell,' Debra mumbled.

'Smell?' said her mother, automatically sniffing the air. 'What smell?'

'The scent,' said Debra, pulling herself to a sitting position. 'I can still smell it. That woman. Who was she?'

'Alice Hall,' said Fiona. 'Why? I can't smell anything. I didn't notice any scent.'

'I did,' said Lori, as she returned with her dad. 'As soon as she came in! Sort of powerful but pleasant. Something unusual about it. Herby.'

'I remember it,' said Debra, screwing her eyes tight shut. 'I know I do. Wherever I was, whatever was happening to me, it was there... that smell.'

Fiona reached out, instinctively, but at the first touch Debra drew away.

'The doctor's on her way,' Lori said, watching Debra fold her arms around herself and start to rock.

Fiona knelt by her daughter, as close as Debra would allow.

'Are you sure?' she asked. 'About the perfume?'

'We've all assumed,' Robert was saying, 'that the abductor's male. But what if it isn't a man? If Debra remembers perfume.'

'Not just any perfume,' Lori said, shivering. 'Hers! Mrs Hall's. I mean what if she's the abductor? She's certainly crazy enough. She's married to a doctor. She'd know a bit about drugs, wouldn't she?'

Fiona took out her mobile. They had to tell the police, that much was certain. But Alice Hall, the abductor? It didn't seem possible somehow.

'She was there, that night, wasn't she?' Lori was saying. 'In The Lion? And her voice is deep enough...just about... to be the voice on the phone calls.'

Fiona nodded as she pressed the number.

'But the police have already talked to her,' Fiona said. 'You know they have. More than once. She popped into

116

The Lion, on the way back from visiting her husband, and had one drink with her sister-in-law. Then they went straight home. They didn't go out again. Her sister-in-law stayed the night. So Alice has an alibi.'

'Unless,' said Robert, 'her sister-in-law lied for her.'

A sudden groan came from Debra. A groan that became a scream as she got up and ran from the room.

Chapter 11

'What happened?' Tonya asked.

'She took an overdose,' Beth whispered. 'Valium. Paracetamol. Locked herself in the bathroom and—'

'Oh, no!' a voice behind them said.

Beth turned to see Simon. Now in the upper sixth.

'How is she?' he said. 'Is she OK? She's not . . .'

'She's in hospital,' said Beth, surprised by the intensity of his reaction.

'Not Debra!' said Tonya, realizing the mistake more quickly than Beth. 'We're not talking about Debra! I mean, would we be standing here if it was Debs?'

'Who then?' said Simon.

'Alice Hall,' said Beth quietly. 'The police went round to interview her and they found her collapsed. Had to break two doors down to get at her.'

Beth was keeping her voice down but she needn't have bothered. The corridor was eerily quiet and empty. Only the sixth form and the new Year 7s were in today. School wouldn't start properly until tomorrow.

'Who's Alice Hall?' said Simon, looking totally confused.

Beth explained as much as she knew, which wasn't a great deal.

'So are you saying,' Simon asked, 'that this woman might be the abductor? That she might have kidnapped

Debs just to get her own back on Mrs Cardew? For running articles in the paper about her husband?'

'I'm saying that Debs thought she recognized the perfume, that's all,' said Beth. 'The police are checking it out. It might not mean anything. They're checking loads of things. Going back over statements. Re-interviewing people. All the ones whose mobiles were stolen and Lori says they've been talking to Tim Simmonds again. With him being a photographer. You know? The pictures the abductor threatened to put on the net?'

'Yeah,' said Simon, seeming to ignore the last bit completely. 'But why would this Mrs Hall OD? If she was innocent?'

'How should I know?' Beth snapped. 'I'm not a detective and neither are you.'

She shook her head, as Simon blushed, looked away.

'I'm sorry,' she said.

'S'all right,' Simon mumbled. 'Anyway, I came to round you up. Mrs Kay's doing an induction talk, in the common room.'

Beth didn't much feel like listening to a talk but she followed Simon anyway. Later they'd be expected to sign up for a whole lot of clubs and sixth form activities. Spend time helping to settle in the Year 7s. Things she'd once looked forward to but which she simply didn't care about anymore.

Fiona lay awake, listening to her husband's snoring, wondering how he could fall asleep so readily. It wouldn't last, she knew. By 3am, he'd be up, pacing around, drinking tea, checking the internet to see if anything had been posted. Even though he knew the police were watching every minute of every day. Robert had been into work for a couple of hours that morning but hadn't been able to concentrate, he'd said, and the Head had suggested he go home.

Not that he'd been able to do much. Debs had been tired and listless. Not washing and showering quite so obsessively but sleeping a lot. Spending the time she was awake staring out of the bedroom window, as though she was expecting someone.

There wasn't much news of Mrs Hall. The police had been able to speak to her but only briefly as she was still too poorly for detailed questioning. Her husband, still on remand, had been allowed out of prison to visit her, under police escort. And, with his help, they'd got her to tell them about the fragrance she was wearing. It wasn't perfume, as such, at all. It was shower gel and talc. Dr Hall's stuff, which his wife had been using because it was there. Because she didn't much care what she was showering with.

For some reason the police weren't saying what exactly it was. Maybe they were going to do some sort of test on Debs later? See if she could pick it out? All they'd said so far was that it was fairly popular. Part of a range of colognes, aftershaves, deodorants, soaps. The sort of product any number of people might use. So where did that leave them?

They couldn't even be sure that Debra's memories were accurate. She could have smelt the scent at any point during that Saturday evening. Or maybe even at the hospital when she was drifting in and out of consciousness. Or not at all. She could have confused it with some other slightly herby smell.

You couldn't convict someone on the strength of a dodgy memory, could you? Mrs Hall, of course, was denying any involvement and a search of her house hadn't revealed anything else. But on the other hand, no photos had appeared on the net while she was in hospital. Not to mention the fact that the police had talked to Mrs Hall's sister-in-law again and she seemed to be changing her story.

The sound of the bedside phone ringing set Fiona's stomach churning. She glanced at the clock as her arm reached out, across her husband. 00:35.

She was too late. Robert had already picked up. Not as deeply asleep, then, as she'd thought.

'Alarm's gone off,' he muttered, passing the phone to her. 'At your office.'

Fiona sighed. It was always happening. They had a high tech security system, which was brilliant for warding off intruders but which could, just as easily, be set off by a passing cat. She was officially still off work, so it wasn't her job to deal with it but, on the other hand, why wake someone else, when there was no chance of her sleeping anyway?

'Right,' she told the security firm. 'I'll deal with it.'

'Be careful,' Robert said, as he always did when she was called out in the middle of the night.

Not that there was any cause for worry. It was simply a matter of driving to the office, turning off the alarm and re-setting it. There wouldn't be an intruder. There never was.

It's not a bluff this time. I've got the photos. And I'm going to use them. In my own time. Just as soon as I get a chance. I mean, why not? They're not anything like as bad as I made out but they'll do. I'll post a couple on the net and pretend they're going to get gradually worse. That should spook them.

Trouble is, I've got to be really careful. I'm good with computers and I think I've figured a way to do it without getting caught. But they're so clever these days, aren't they? With their tracking. They reckon they're closing the net on all the heavy porn guys. They say there'll be thousands more arrests over the next year or so. Gaols are going to be full of them, by the sound of things. Hackers too. It's not so easy for them anymore either. But there are always ways to beat the system, if you're smart enough. And I'm definitely that.

Can't help wondering if I've gone a bit over-the-top in trying to throw everyone off the scent, as it were. Protesting too much methinks. It's Shakespeare, that. Hamlet or is it Macbeth? Doesn't matter. I think I've got the quote wrong anyway. And that's not the point. The point is . . .

I don't know. Haven't a clue. My head's all over the place. Not to mention my stomach. I don't feel too good. Not good at all. I've been stupid again. Overdoing it. But there's no one around to stop me now, is there? No one to help me put the brakes on. No one to moan at me. So I'm off again. Pushing the self-destruct button. Just when I need a clear head. Because she knows something. She definitely knows something. But how much?

Oh God, my head's anything but clear. I keep getting mixed up about what I've said to who. And what I've heard. The scent! Why would Debra remember a smell of all things? I never thought of that. But I should have done. I should have been more careful. Has she remembered it properly? Will she pick it out in a test? Will she recognize the truth if it stares her in the face. Funny that, see. It's called Truth. Calvin Klein's Truth. Not my usual. But that's what I'd been using. Still, it doesn't matter. Completely circumstantial, isn't it? There must be dozens of similar products. It's not real evidence, is it? And besides, there's nothing . . .

Nothing? What? What was I thinking? I don't know. Every-thing's getting all muddled again. These latest developments. They've got me all confused. And who knows what I might say or do when I get all mixed up like this? Might end up blurting something out. Because that's another thing. It's weird. I don't understand it. But part of me still wants to tell. Shout it out. Tell them all what I've done and why. Guilty conscience? I don't think so. Because none of it was my fault. Not really. Cry for help? Hardly. It's not me that needs help, is it? I'm fine. I don't have a problem.

Fiona checked the front door to the office. Nothing amiss there. No sign of entry, forced or otherwise. On the other side of the street a couple walking past slowed, listening to the blare of the alarm, wondering what was happening, before hurrying on. What, Fiona thought, was the point of having buildings and cars alarmed, when no one took any notice anyway? In the old days they'd had a night caretaker but he'd disappeared in one of the many rounds of job cuts so now they had to put up with this sort of thing every few weeks.

She went round the back. Looked, paused, looked again. Was it her imagination or was the door not quite closed? She gave it a gentle push and it swung open. But it hadn't been forced. The lock was still intact.

It was possible that one of the journalists had been covering a night job and popped into the office. But if they'd used their key card, why had the alarm gone off? And if they'd managed to trip the alarm, whilst in the building, why hadn't they simply switched it off?

She stepped back, looked up and saw a light in one of the second floor offices. Colleague or intruder? Best not to take chances. Best to phone the police. OK ... next thing, turn the alarm off. The noise was really doing her head in.

The back door led into a narrow entrance hall with stairs immediately in front and the alarm corner right. It was an old building, damp, cold and quite dark even now she'd switched the light on. Fiona suddenly shivered, as her fingers fumbled with the alarm code. She had the crazy feeling someone was watching her. She looked behind her. Nothing. She looked up at the stairs. No one.

Imagination, she told herself, as she finally turned off the alarm. She'd done the same thing before, dozens of times, without a second thought. But now, after what had happened to Debs, she was jumpy, edgy. Her mind was all over the place, wondering whether someone might have set off the alarm deliberately, to lure her here.

Mad as the idea obviously was, she decided not to hang around. She'd wait in the car until the police arrived. Maybe phone Robert. Talk to someone. Get her mind away from wild imaginings. But the sudden noise, immediately above her, wasn't imagination.

She looked up, saw the figure at the top of the stairs, just before it started to sway and came crashing down.

Debra was floating again. Only it didn't feel safe this time. It felt wobbly, scary, as though she was going to fall at any minute. But she had to stay up there. Watching the girl below. Trying to see the details. The room, garage, storehouse, whatever it was. She knew she was dreaming. Wanted to dream. Because only in her dreams did she ever get close. And even that wasn't close enough. Everything was cloudy, misty. Nothing would come into focus. Sometimes she heard a door opening. Sometimes she even saw a figure. But it wouldn't take shape. Develop the features she wanted to see.

It must be there somewhere. In her head. All the memories. All the information. If only she could stay up here long enough. She'd see something. Some clue. Or maybe she didn't want to. Didn't want to see. Maybe she already knew but wouldn't let herself admit it. That's why she was up here! Distanced. Remote. Too far away from herself. Of course she'd never see like that! She had to let herself go back. Be Debra again. Feel what she'd felt. See what she'd seen. Face the pain. Face all of it.

Do it, Debra. Do it now. Slip down, slowly, gently. Don't be scared. Go down there with her.

'No! Don't do that. Don't hurt me. Please don't hurt me.'

It's not real, Debra. It's not real anymore. Don't push it away. Bring the figure towards you. Bring it back. Hear the breathing. So close. So very close. See the figure bending over you. That scent. That scent again.

'Leave me alone! Don't touch me!'

Stop it, Debra. Stop fighting it. Open your mind. Open your eyes. Bring it into focus. See the face. You *did* see it, Debra. You know you did. Let yourself look again. Just one glimpse. You know who it is.

Light touch of icy fingers on her arm. Debra opened her eyes. Saw the figure standing over her and screamed.

'Debs!' said Robert Cardew, switching on the light. 'Debs, are you . . .'

'I'm sorry,' said Lori, as Debra's eyes focused and her screams subsided. 'I'm sorry. I woke up when the phone rang. Heard Mum's car driving off.'

'Security alarm again,' her father said.

Lori nodded.

'Then I heard Debs shouting out. I came in. She was thrashing around. Shouting. I didn't know what to do.

126

Whether to wake her. I'm sorry, Debs. I didn't mean to scare you. Debs? Debs, are you OK?'

Debra's eyes were flicking rapidly, starting to roll back in her head. Colour was draining from her face as though she was about to pass out.

'I think I know,' she said quietly. 'I think I know who it was.'

Chapter 12

'Oh no!' Fiona murmured, as she knelt by Tim, trying to avoid the sharp splinters of glass that surrounded him.

She didn't know how she'd managed to get out of the way of the falling figure but she had. Instinctively. And there'd been nothing to break his fall. A lump was swelling rapidly on his forehead, his right hand was bleeding where the bottle had sliced in and his left arm was twisted awkwardly beneath him. Should she try to move him? No. Best wait for the ambulance. They should be here any second. And the police. Where were they? It seemed ages since she'd phoned but it probably wasn't.

Tim groaned. The first sound he'd made since he fell.

'It's all right,' she said.

The same meaningless words that she'd said to Debra over and over.

'Just keep still,' she said, trying not to retch at the smell of whisky that was everywhere.

She was kneeling in a puddle of the stuff and vaguely wondered how much he'd drunk. What had set him off on a binge again. How long he'd been there. How many bottles they'd find upstairs.

'Snottlewhite,' he was mumbling. 'S'notallright.'

'Ssssh,' she soothed.

'No,' he said. 'Youdontunderstand.'

With the words mumbled and run together, Fiona

didn't. Was barely listening. Concentrating on trying to stop the bleeding from his hand, she let him ramble on in his drunken, half-concussed stupor. Until a word, a name, caught her attention.

'What?' she said.

'Debra,' he said. 'Remembers. Mustremember. Debraknows.'

'Knows what?' said Fiona.

Tim stared at her, his bloodshot eyes leaking tears.

'Me,' he said, as his eyes started to close. 'Wasme.'

'What was you?' she asked again, lifting his head, supporting it. 'What are you saying?'

'Pills,' he muttered, his eyes briefly opening, then shutting again.

Words dragged out, painfully slowly this time, as he started to slip away.

'I . . . gave . . . her . . . it . . . was . . . me.'

His head thudded on the bare floor as Fiona let it drop. Her eyes rested, for a moment on the broken, jagged end of the whisky bottle, lying next to his hand. She picked it up as she rose to her feet. Staggered backwards, not wanting to be near him. Looked at the bottle again. Wanted to smash it down into his face, cutting, ripping, gouging. Unable to stop herself, she lurched forward, felt her arm slamming down, just as someone gripped her and pulled her back.

'I don't want it,' Debra said, as the doctor prepared the sedative. 'Where's Mum? Why isn't she back? I want Mum. I want to tell her.'

'She'll be back soon,' said Lori, sitting on the bed, next to Debra. 'Now, please. Have the sedative, Debs. You need to sleep. Real sleep.'

Debra nodded and Lori gave her a hug, before standing back to let the doctor do his job. It was only a quick hug but Debra hadn't squirmed, cried out or tried to pull away, so that had to be progress, didn't it? That and the way she'd let Dad hold her hand, as they'd waited for the doctor.

They'd felt a bit guilty about calling the doctor out. Because, after the initial outburst, when they thought Debra was going into some kind of fit, Debs had settled down and by the time the doctor had arrived, she was fine. Utterly drained. Utterly exhausted. But in better spirits than they'd seen her since she came home.

She hadn't actually remembered anything definite. No name, no face, nothing concrete. But she'd been close, she said. Close enough to know the memory was there. Close enough to believe that she could reach it. Maybe with the help of hypnotherapy.

That, in itself, was progress. When hypnosis had been tentatively mentioned previously, Debs had gone wild. Claimed she didn't want anybody messing about with her again. Messing inside her head. Besides, she'd said, there was no point. There was nothing there. Nothing there to find. Now, suddenly, she seemed so much more positive. So much more confident about facing things. Utterly determined to drag the memories from wherever they lay buried.

'Do you think this is real progress?' her dad was asking the doctor, as Debra drifted off to sleep. 'Or just the effect of the dream she had? Do you think, when she wakes up, we might be back to square one?'

'No,' said the doctor. 'Not from what you've told me. It's very early days. The healing process can take months. Sometimes even years. But it looks as though she's made a start.'

Lori felt a smile settling on her lips as her dad showed the doctor out. A real smile. Not the false, fixed kind that they'd all got so used to wearing recently. But a real one that came from inside. She felt ridiculously happy. Euphoric almost. Out of all proportion, she knew. As if someone had suddenly released a valve and all the tension, all the pain of the last couple of weeks was gushing away. She couldn't wait to tell Mum about the hug!

She looked at her watch. Come to think of it, Debs was right. Mum should be back by now. She heard her dad close the front door. Then the phone rang.

On Wednesday, the first real day of term, Robert Cardew wasn't in school but the news had got round anyway. Within seconds of her arrival, a dozen people had rushed up to Beth, telling her what Lori had already told her when she'd phoned earlier that morning. Information that hadn't exactly surprised Beth but which she still found difficult to take in.

'They've got him!' someone announced.

'It's that photographer, Tim Simmonds,' someone else said.

How did they know? Beth wondered. How did news spread so fast? The radio report had only said that a man had been arrested in connection with the abduction of Debra Cardew. No name had been mentioned and certainly no details. Yet everyone seemed to know about the drama of the previous night. How Tim had confessed to Debra's mum before he passed out.

'How's Debs?' said Tonya, dragging Beth away from the crowds. 'How's she taken it? I mean she liked the guy, didn't she? Trusted him?'

'She doesn't know yet,' said Beth. 'The doctor gave her a sedative and she's still spark out. I just hope it doesn't set her back again, when she finds out. Lori seemed to think Debs made some sort of breakthrough last night.'

'What sort of breakthrough?' Tonya asked, as Beth's mobile rang.

'Shit!' said Beth, darting into the sixth form common room.

It was the only place they were allowed to use their phones.

'Hi,' she said. 'Yes. Yes it's true. I know. Oh! I'm sorry. Yeah, it must be.'

Beth clutched the phone closer to her ear, looked at Tonya, shook her head.

'I don't know,' Beth said. 'What time? I think so. I'll try. I'm sure it'll sort itself out. Yeah. See ya!'

She couldn't help the few tears which came to her eyes, as she switched the phone off and started rummaging in her bag for her new timetable.

'Miriam?' Tonya asked.

Beth nodded.

'Don't suppose you're free last period, are you?' Beth said.

'No,' said Tonya. 'I've got chemistry all afternoon. Why?'

'Miriam's a bit upset,' Beth said. 'Well, more than a bit. Removal men are due any minute and her mum's had some sort of bust up with Eddie.'

'Eddie,' said Tonya. 'Why?'

'I don't know,' said Beth. 'I noticed some tension between them at Miriam's party, though. Miriam says it's something to do with Uncle Gordon and the time Eddie was away travelling but she's not sure what. Her mum won't tell her and, to make things worse, her dad sided with Eddie, apparently. Accused her mum of being completely blind where Gordon's concerned and... anyway, with all the rows, they got behind with the move and they're not likely to get away before three, so I said I'd pop round, try to see her before she goes.'

'Well give her my love,' said Tonya. 'Tell her I hope it all gets sorted out. And wish her luck with the new school.'

All right. It's not as bad as it seems. It's not as bad as it seems. Clear my head and keep my mouth shut. Till I've thought it all out. Worked it through. Or have I said too much already? No. It doesn't matter, does it? What I've said? There's no real evidence. I keep telling myself that. I made sure. So, rule number one . . . whatever anyone asks, deny it. Play the victim. Outraged innocence and all that. Stick to the stories I've told all along. If

133

the worst comes to the worst it's only her word against mine, isn't it? And she's hardly impartial, is she? Never liked me much. I can prove that. If I have to. Might not even have to. Might not ever get that far. If I stay calm. Whatever she thinks she heard, whatever she thinks she knows, it doesn't matter, does it?

The photos are safe. That's one good thing. No one's ever going to find my little hiding place. And I might still be able to find a use for them. A very good use for them, in fact. If I'm careful, if I keep what's left of my head. There's something. . . something going on that I don't understand. But I can make it work for me. I'm sure I can.

Beth hurried out of the school gates, cursing under her breath. She was late. Mr Mason had nabbed her in the corridor, droning on about a mix-up in the timetable and group sizes. How she'd have to change from history in option block 2 to history in 5, then do Lit in 3 and switch IT to 2. As if she cared!

Then he'd started talking about something she did care about. Debra. And she'd felt obliged to stay, answering his questions. So now it was almost half past three and though Miriam's was only round the corner, she could well have missed her.

Had missed her. She could see the house now and there were no removal vans outside. No cars either. She walked up anyway. Just in case one of the cars was still in the garage. In case someone was still around.

The garage door was shut but the front door was open slightly.

'Miriam?'

No answer.

Beth moved through the empty hallway and jumped as the lounge door swung open.

'Sorry,' Eddie muttered. 'Didn't mean to scare you. You've just missed them. Miriam and her dad went off a couple of minutes ago. Auntie Jill went earlier. Ahead of the removal men. I was just about to go myself. I said I'd drop the keys with the estate agent. New people aren't due till tomorrow.'

It was quite a long speech for Eddie. He was talking rapidly, looking as uptight and anxious as always. She wondered whether he'd made up with Miriam's mum before she left, but didn't like to ask.

'How's your friend?' he asked. 'How's Debra?'

'OK,' she said. 'Not too bad. Making a bit of progress, they reckon.'

'That's good,' said Eddie, smiling. 'Miriam's been really worried about her. I mean, we all have. But at least they've caught him now. At least that's something.'

Beth nodded.

'You don't look very sure,' said Eddie. 'You don't think they've got it wrong, do you? Arrested the wrong person? I know Miriam was shocked. Kept saying she didn't believe it.'

'Oh, I can believe it all right,' Beth snapped. 'All the time Debs was missing, my mind kept going back to him. The way he was acting with her at the school. All sort of smarmy and over familiar. Then the way he lost it with

135

her in the pub that night. I knew it was him. I knew it was him all along. I even told the police what I thought. And now I just keep thinking I should have pushed it more. Made them believe me. Made them take it seriously. Then they might have found her earlier. And she might not have had to go through...whatever happened, whatever he did, whatever sleazy, sick photographs he took.'

'It wasn't your fault!' Eddie said. 'You couldn't have changed anything, could you?'

'I think I could,' said Beth. 'That's the trouble. If not about Tim Simmonds, then earlier, at the party. If I'd kept an eye on her better. But you never think, do you? You never think it's going to happen.'

Eddie was shaking his head and Beth wondered why she was blurting it all out like this. Now. To a person she barely knew. Because she had to tell someone? Let it all out some way, somehow.

'I'm sorry,' she said. 'It's just that I feel so angry all the time. I mean, I know he's confessed and everything but what if he gets away with it? He's only got to deny it, hasn't he? What can they prove? He was drunk, concussed, so maybe he didn't know what he was saying. Or Mrs Cardew might have misheard. Any decent lawyer could tear the case apart, couldn't they?'

'Not if they find other evidence,' said Eddie. 'Maybe they'll find the photos he threatened to use. That's possible, isn't it?'

'Or perhaps there'll be something to link him to that

fragrance Debs keeps going on about,' said Beth. 'Maybe he wears the same stuff that Mrs Hall was wearing. Or something similar.'

'Mmm,' said Eddie thoughtfully. 'That's a point.'

But even as Beth had been saying it, she'd realized there was something odd. A loose end. Something that didn't quite connect.

'What's wrong?' Eddie asked.

Chapter 13

'Are you crazy?' Debra screamed. 'Have you all gone completely mad? Tim Simmonds? You think Tim abducted me! Hurt me like that? Almost bloody killed me! No way. No way at all!'

'I know it's difficult,' her dad said.

'Not difficult!' Debra yelled at him. 'Impossible. Completely impossible.'

'Debs, stop it!' said Lori. 'And listen!'

'I've listened,' said Debra.

'It wasn't just me who heard him,' her mother said quietly. 'He said it again, when he arrived at the hospital. To a nurse. With two police officers standing there!'

'Shut up!' said Debra, standing up, walking around the room. 'Let me think. Let me think. How can I make sense of anything with you all going on at me all the time?'

As Debra stood up, Fiona sat down, resting her head in her hands. She was exhausted. Her head was throbbing. Words, his words, kept screaming in her head. And, worse than anything, the image of herself, the broken bottle in her hand. She was going to do it. She was really going to do it. If that police officer hadn't dragged her back, she'd have smashed the bottle right into Tim's face. She would have attacked an unconscious man. Her! With all her pacifist principles. Someone who'd never hit anyone in

138

her life. Never so much as tapped her kids. Last night she'd wanted to kill a man. She still did.

Tim hadn't retracted his confession since he'd come round properly. But then he hadn't confirmed it either. In fact he hadn't said anything. Not a word. As if he didn't know where he was or who was speaking to him. He was in shock, the police said. Shock! They were all in shock.

'Tell me again!' Debra demanded. 'Tell me exactly what he said last night.'

Fiona sat up. She hadn't the strength to go through it all again. But she did. Watching Debra's eyes flickering rapidly as she listened.

'He didn't mean me!' Debra said, as soon as her mother finished.

Fiona shook her head. What could she possibly say? Debra was in denial. Still groggy from the sedative. They'd told her at the wrong time. It was all too soon.

'He said your name, Debs,' Lori pointed out quietly. 'Of course he meant you.'

'He said I knew something,' said Debra. 'And he was right. I do. I've heard it all before. All those things he said to Mum. He's made the same confession before. To me!'

Lori glanced at her parents, who were both shaking their heads.

'He was talking about Evie!' Debra said.

'No, Debs,' her dad said. 'I'm sorry but—'

'Do you remember?' Debra said. 'A few months back. Not long after Evie died. I was out with Marc. We'd had another row and he stormed off.'

Her dad looked bewildered.

'Yes you do!' Debra insisted. 'Because I phoned you and asked you to come and pick me up. And when you turned up, Tim was with me, slumped on that bench outside the bank.'

'Right,' said her dad. 'Yes. I'm with you, now. And I ended up driving him home.'

'Yeah,' said Debra. 'Well, what I didn't tell you was that when Tim first staggered up to me, he was crying. Going on about Evie. About how she'd wanted to die with dignity. Or with whatever dignity she had left.'

'OK,' said her dad thoughtfully. 'But—'

'He told me he'd helped her to die,' said Debra quietly. 'Given her the pills. Held the glass of water to her lips.'

'Is this true?' said Fiona.

'Of course it's bloody true!' said Debra.

'Why didn't you tell us?' said Lori.

'I don't know,' said Debra, shaking her head. 'He was drunk. I thought he might be confused. Then I thought, if it really was the truth, he might get into trouble. It's illegal, isn't it? To help someone to die like that? But it's not wrong! He hadn't done anything wrong! He loved her. She was dying anyway! It was what she wanted! He gave her the pills but she took them herself. It was her choice!'

'Oh my God,' said Fiona, letting the words from the previous night come back to her, slowly and clearly. 'It could be. Everything he said. I don't know. It could be. I never thought. Never imagined. But he could have done. He could have meant Evie.'

140

'It's all going to come out now,' said Debra, starting to cry. 'He'll get into trouble whatever happens. But he didn't hurt me. It wasn't Tim. I know it wasn't.'

Fiona walked across to the phone. They had to tell the police what they knew. Now. Straight away. It wasn't conclusive. There was still a chance that Tim had become so unhinged over Evie, got everything so completely twisted in his mind that he'd abducted Debs. But if not? If Debra was right. If it wasn't Tim. If he wasn't the abductor, where did that leave them?

Back to Debra's vague memory of a fragrance? Back to Alice Hall? It was possible. The sister-in-law had been giving the police a lot of new information. Things she hadn't bothered to mention before. About Alice's periods of depression. Several of them, over the years. Even before the trouble with her husband. Alice had always been a bit unstable, the sister-in-law had said. And, yes, they'd had an early night after their drink at The Lion so it just might have been possible for Alice to sneak out again, without her sister-in-law waking.

Tim or Alice? Last night Fiona had been so certain, now she was totally confused again. But at least it was a relief to know that both of them were, at the moment, still under close supervision in hospital.

'Whisky,' said Beth. 'You'd think if Debs was going to remember a smell from Tim it would be whisky. Or body odour. That's what I remember about him. Not cologne or soap or anything like that. I don't think personal

141

hygiene has been high on his agenda for quite a while.'

'Maybe it wasn't a fragrance as such at all,' said Eddie. 'Miriam said Debs had described it as a herby smell.'

'Yes,' said Beth.

'So perhaps he was keeping her near a garden or an allotment or something,' Eddie pointed out. 'Could even have been someone growing dope, like that Stefan.'

It sounded a bit far fetched to Beth and she was sure Stefan had been eliminated from enquiries but then Eddie was sharper than he looked. And he'd been right once before, when she'd doubted him. About the stolen mobiles.

'Ever thought of becoming a cop?' Beth asked.

Eddie looked a bit hurt, as though he thought she was mocking him.

'It *could* have been real herbs,' he said. 'Then the smell of that Truth stuff just brought it back. Reminded her. I mean it's a very outdoor sort of smell, isn't it?'

'I don't know,' said Beth vacantly.

She glanced at her watch. They could stand here all night speculating but it wouldn't do any good. And besides it was getting late. Mum got completely paranoid these days if she was so much as a couple of seconds overdue. She moved towards the door. Paused.

There was something about what Eddie had just said that was niggling at her. No. It was stupid. She was being edgy, paranoid, like Mum. Like everyone else these days.

Eddie had moved alongside her, his hand on the

door, ready to show her out. He smiled as she looked at him.

'You OK?' he asked.

'Yeah,' she said. 'I'm fine. It's nothing. I was just thinking about that fragrance Debs smelt on Mrs Hall. What did you say it was called?'

'Oh that,' said Eddie. 'Truth! Yeah, I thought it was a bit ironic too. I mean it's the one thing we might never really know, isn't it?'

'Mmm,' said Beth again as she prepared to edge past, overwhelmed by the sudden feeling that she knew exactly that.

The truth.

'Who was that?' Debra asked as her dad put the phone down.

'Beth's mum,' he said. 'Asking if Beth was here. She hasn't turned up from school yet.'

'It's only twenty past four,' said Lori, glancing at the clock.

'I know,' said her dad. 'But Beth's mobile's off. And her mum's getting a bit worked up.'

'Has she checked the school?' Mrs Cardew said. 'Maybe Beth's stayed behind.'

'No she left early,' said Robert. 'Tonya reckoned Beth was popping round to see Miriam. But, of course, the phones are off there and they can't reach Miriam's mobile. I've got some stuff I ought to take into school. I could do it now, I suppose. Stop by at Miriam's. Just check. Tell Beth to phone her mum, if she's still there.'

Nobody argued. Nobody suggested that he was overreacting. That Beth was only a few minutes late. They all understood how her mother would feel.

'I'll come with you,' Debra said. 'I can phone her mum, tell her what we're doing and keep trying Beth's mobile while you're driving.'

'If you're sure,' said her dad.

Debra wasn't. But she grabbed her jacket and bag anyway. She'd do it. She'd have to leave the house sometime. Couldn't lock herself away for ever. She knew that. So she may as well do it now. When she had a reason. Not that there was any real need to panic. This was bound to be a false alarm. Beth was probably walking up her front path right now. Opening the door. Beth's mum would phone any minute to say she was back. Then perhaps they could drive round there. Go and see her.

If she could get herself out of the door that was. Her dad was holding it open, waiting for her. She edged forward. Looked right and left along the street. It was empty and more reassuringly familiar than she'd expected.

It was only a few steps to the car. She could do it. She knew she could. Knew she must. She clutched her dad's hand, almost dragging him forward, pulled open the passenger door with her other hand and slid in. Held onto the seat, breathing deeply, as the car pulled out of the drive.

She was outside. Facing the world again. Slowly, she let go of the seat, pulled her mobile out, called Beth.

144

She had to answer, she had to. Debra couldn't wait to tell her that she was out of the house and on her way to see her!

'Are you all right, Beth?' Eddie was asking. 'You look really pale.'

'Yeah,' said Beth. 'I'm fine. I have to go.'

'You don't really look well enough,' he said. 'Let me get you a drink. I think there's a bottle of water lying around somewhere.'

'No,' said Beth, her voice tight and hoarse.

Eddie's hand was still on the door. Beth looked up the hallway, towards the kitchen. Maybe she should make a dash for it. Run out the back. But what if the back door was locked? She didn't want to spook him. Let him know she was onto something. Or did he know already? Was that why he was guarding the door? Or was she being crazy? There was probably a logical explanation. Eddie didn't look dangerous. In fact, he looked concerned. Genuinely concerned.

'Are you going to tell me what's wrong?' he asked.

'It's nothing,' she said.

He smiled at her, unfreezing the fear. What was she thinking of? Eddie hadn't abducted Debs. What possible reason could he have? It was Tim. She'd known it was Tim all along and now he'd even confessed, for goodness' sake! What more proof did she need?

'It's stupid,' she added. 'Look, could you just open the door?'

145

'Sure,' he said, opening it, standing back a pace. 'Now are you going to tell me what this is about?'

'I think I've been reading too many thrillers,' said Beth, relieved that she could see the outside world, that she no longer felt trapped.

Eddie looked lost, bemused, as he often did.

Beth stepped outside. Turned to face him. Remembered how he'd been out searching for Debs. Remembered his 'string 'em up' diatribe at Miriam's party. Not to mention the lead he'd given the police about the stolen mobiles. Were any of those the actions of a kidnapper? How could she possibly have thought, even for a moment, that Eddie was involved?

Did she owe him an explanation? Probably. Even if he ended up thinking she was a total eejit.

'The name of the fragrance,' Beth said hurriedly, 'that Debs thought she recognized. Lori said the police weren't releasing it but I guess they must have done.'

Confusion again on Eddie's face.

'Because you knew what it was called,' Beth added.

'Oh!' said Eddie. 'Right. Yeah. Well, I was just going from what Miriam told me. Might not even be right. You know how rumours get round.'

Beth nodded, started to move.

'But,' said Eddie slowly, 'you thought ...'

'I'm not sure what I thought,' said Beth. 'Like I said, too many thrillers. You know, criminal lets something slip by accident.'

'I'm not a criminal,' Eddie snapped.

146

'I know,' said Beth.

'So why does everybody treat me like one?' Eddie said, his face flaring red and angry.

'I'm sorry,' said Beth. 'I wasn't suggesting...'

'Weren't you?' said Eddie. 'Just because I knew the name of the stupid scent. Just because I'd heard the same rumour as everyone else. Maybe you think I'm a pervert like my dad, is that it?'

'No!' said Beth.

'Why not?' said Eddie. 'Everybody else seems to.'

It took Beth a moment to realize what he meant, what was making him so angry.

'You mean all the hate mail and stuff?' said Beth. 'Yeah, I know...'

'No. No you don't!' he said. 'You don't know anything. You don't know what it's like. All I want to do is forget about it all, get on with life. But *they* won't let me. *She* won't let me.'

'Who?' said Beth, totally confused.

'Everyone!' said Eddie. 'The people who send the hate mail. The flaming newspapers. Dredging it all up every time there's a new case. And now her. Auntie Jill! She reckons it was me who accessed those porn sites, you know. Not my dad at all. That my dad covered up for me, even went to gaol for me, she says! Anything to protect his precious son! She's threatening to tell the police. I mean it's stupid, isn't it? She's bluffing. They'd never believe her.'

Eddie laughed. A short, manic snort, prompting Beth to take another step away from him.

147

'She's never liked me,' Eddie said, almost to himself. 'Couldn't believe her brother would do something like that, so it had to be me, didn't it?'

'And was it?' said Beth.

'No!' said Eddie. 'And anyway, what if it was? What does it matter? Why does everybody make such a big deal out of it? It's not as though you're hurting anyone, is it? It's only pictures.'

'Pictures of children,' Beth pointed out. 'Real children! Being abused! It's not a victimless crime, is it, Eddie? The pictures are photographs not bloody paintings. This is real kids we're talking about.'

'Little innocents, eh?' sneered Eddie. 'Just like you. On the front page of the paper, weren't you? You and Debra. Flashing your legs and tits for the camera!'

The way he spat the word Debra made Beth feel suddenly sick. Eddie's face had contorted into a cross between a snarl and a leer. Was this the face of someone who liked looking at children? The face of someone who'd let his own father go to gaol for him? The face of Debra's abductor?

'What?' said Eddie, edging towards her. 'What now?'

'Nothing, it's nothing,' said Beth.

She was shaking her head but knew her eyes were giving a completely different message. She had to get away. Quick.

Before she could make a move, Eddie lunged forward, grabbed her arm and pulled her back inside.

Chapter 14

Beth was swung round so that her back smashed against the door as it slammed shut, leaving her bent double, gasping for breath. As she straightened, lifting her head, preparing to scream, a hand was clamped over her mouth and Eddie's full weight pressed against her, pinning her back as he spoke.

'Don't scream,' he said. 'Don't move.'

Oh, God, what have I done? What am I going to do? I shouldn't have panicked! That stupid Simmonds bloke has confessed. I could have used that. If I'd kept calm. I shouldn't have let Beth rattle me. She didn't know anything. Not for certain. But it's too late now.

Beth tried to push forward, cry out, but he was too strong for her. His hand pressed down harder over her mouth and nose, his other hand crept up, grasping her throat, making it impossible to breathe.

Do it. Do it. Finish it off. No! Don't be crazy. You can't get away with it. Not this. But if I don't? She'll tell them. They'll start snooping round again. I've got nothing to lose. Nothing at all.

Beth felt her body sagging, dissolving, her eyes squeezing shut against her will.

Then the ring of the doorbell. The ring that made Eddie jump and momentarily lose his grip, sending Beth slumping to the floor.

'Hello? Who's in there? Who is that? What's going on?'

'Miriam? Beth? Is that you?'

The first voice male, deep. The second Debra's! Even through the whirling, dizzying sickness of her head, her stomach, Beth knew it was Debra and called out in response.

Her call was faint, barely audible but a second was impossible. Eddie had dropped down beside her, pulling something from the pocket of his jeans, snapping it open. Knife. He'd got a knife! Penknife or camping knife. Not large but big enough to make Beth freeze as its cold blade traced a light path along her chest, up her throat, stroking the flesh on her chin, her cheek.

'Please,' Beth whispered, as someone banged on the door. 'Please don't hurt me.'

'Open it,' Debra was screaming. 'Open the door. Beth? Can you hear me? Beth!'

The clatter of the letterbox, a gasp, another scream, high-pitched, hysterical.

'Dad, she's in there. With Eddie Wilcox! What's he doing? What's happening? He's got a knife. Call the police. Tell them he's got a knife!'

They're calling the cops already! Tricky. But I'm all right. I've got my hostage, haven't I? Lucky I didn't get carried away. Lucky I didn't squeeze too tight. They're not going to touch me while I've still got her alive, are they?

'That's right,' Eddie called. 'I've got a knife. So move back or your friend gets her pretty face cut, OK? Any trouble and I'll slit her throat.'

Would I? Would I do that? Could I? It's shut them up,

anyway, for the time being. So what now? Get out of here. Out the back? Before the cops arrive?

'Stand up,' he said, pressing the point of the knife under Beth's right ear. 'Stand up!'

Outside Robert Cardew clung on to Debra, as she sobbed and shook in his arms, all the time trying to pull away.

'You can't do anything,' he said, holding tighter. 'We can't get in there. If you spook him, Beth'll get hurt. We have to wait. Do you understand?'

Debra nodded, aware, for the first time, that they weren't alone. That neighbours, passers-by had started to gather, alerted by the screams, the fuss.

'We'll go round the back,' she heard one man say.

'Don't try to stop him,' her father warned. 'The police said to wait for them. Not to tackle him. Not while he's got Beth.'

'Where are they?' said Debra. 'Why aren't they here? What's happening? Why's Eddie doing this?'

The click. The sudden connection, which she hadn't made in her initial panic.

'Was it him? Eddie. Who drugged me? It can't have been. Why would he? Why me? Why Beth? Dad! We've got to do something.'

'It's all right,' her dad said. 'They're here.'

No sirens, no warning. Just cars, marked and unmarked pulling up, quietly, outside Miriam's old house and an ambulance standing by.

★

151

'They love all this, don't they?' said Eddie, looking out of the kitchen window at the people standing in the back garden. 'You know what they'd like, don't you?'

Beth didn't answer. The knife was pressing against her back now, she didn't want to take any chances, say the wrong thing.

'Don't you?' Eddie asked again, squeezing her arm.

Beth shook her head.

'They'd like me to kill you,' he said. 'That's what they're waiting for. The drama, the action. They'd pretend to be horrified but they'd love it!'

'No,' Beth whispered.

'Oh, it's all right,' said Eddie. 'I'm not going to do it. Not unless I have to. We're going to walk out of here, you and me. And there's nothing they can do to stop us. Back or front, it doesn't make any difference. Front, I think. Why not?'

He pushed her round, marching her back through the kitchen, into the hall.

'Why?' Beth forced herself to say.

The police must surely be here by now. If she could just keep him talking. Give them a bit more time to get into position, make plans, do whatever they were going to do.

'Why did you kidnap Debs? Why her?'

He laughed.

'Because I wanted to,' he said. 'Because I wanted to mess up the Cardews' lives like they messed up mine.'

'How?' Beth asked. 'How had they messed up your life?'

Eddie swung her round to face him, the knife held low, near her abdomen.

'Don't you read the local paper?' he snarled. 'Mrs Cardew's paper. Didn't you see the things they wrote about my dad? Calling him a paedophile. Stirring up trouble. If you thought the stuff Miriam got was bad, you should have seen what I had to put up with! Bricks through the window, car tyres slashed, dog muck through the letterbox and all because of Fiona bloody Cardew!'

He believed it, Beth thought, trying to keep her face neutral, trying not to show the anger, fear, disgust that was forcing its way through every pore. It was all someone else's fault. Not his.

'But the phone,' Beth said. 'You claimed your mobile was stolen at the party! With the others.'

'Yeah, clever that, wasn't it?' said Eddie, smiling.

'And the way you went on at Marc, at Miriam's that night!'

'Another diversion,' said Eddie, the smile fading. 'A bit of drama. A bit of play acting. But I was right, wasn't I? I said if they didn't stop him, some other girl might not be so lucky.'

'You don't have to do this,' whispered Beth. 'You could give yourself up. Get help.'

'I've had help,' he said, leaning into her, his breath warm on her face.

She tried to edge back but he held on to her.

153

'What do you mean?' she asked, looking at the door, hoping that something was happening out there.

'After I messed up at University,' he said, his eyes looking somehow through her, beyond her.

'Messed up?' said Beth. 'You didn't mess up! Miriam told me you got a first!'

'Oh yeah,' said Eddie. 'I got my first. Well I had to, didn't I? Nothing but the best. That's what Dad expected. That's why he'd spent all that money on my education. So he could brag about me to his friends on the council. Even the first wasn't good enough, though.'

Why am I telling her all this? What do I expect? Sympathy?

'Dad wanted me to stay on. Do an MA. And I was going to. Until my landlady's daughter started telling tales about what we'd been up to.'

Beth stared at him, not daring to ask how old the girl was. She didn't have to. Eddie had read the question in her eyes and was already answering it.

'Yeah, she was under age,' said Eddie. 'So what? She wasn't a kid! She was fourteen. She knew exactly what she was doing. And it's not as though we actually had sex or anything! I can't...I mean...anyway it doesn't matter. We just...'

'Don't,' said Beth, glancing at the door again. 'Don't tell me. I don't want to know.'

'It was nothing,' said Eddie. 'But her mother made a big deal out of it. Got in touch with my dad.'

'And what happened?' Beth asked, wondering whether he'd been on the sex offenders' register, whether the

154

police had somehow missed it.

'Dad paid them off,' laughed Eddie. 'It's amazing what people will do for money. How their stories suddenly change. But Dad wouldn't leave it at that. Said I needed help. Said I was sick! Blamed the exam pressure. So he sent me "travelling", didn't he? To a clinic abroad. So people wouldn't find out.'

'And did anyone else know about all this?' said Beth. 'Did Miriam know?'

Eddie drew back a fraction. Shook his head.

'No, Dad kept it quiet. Well, he would, wouldn't he? And after the clinic, I really did go travelling.'

Eddie laughed again.

'Maybe I went to the wrong places. Got into some bad habits. Things Dad couldn't even imagine! He thought I was sorted, see? When I got back. He was dead pleased when I joined the business. Until the police came knocking on the door. About those porn sites!'

'But why take the blame for you?' asked Beth. 'Why did your dad take the blame?'

'Cops thought it was him,' said Eddie, shrugging. 'It was his credit card I'd been using, see? I never asked him to lie for me, he just did. Maybe he thought he was giving me another chance. Maybe it was love. Guilt.'

'Guilt?' said Beth.

'For pushing me too hard all the time. I don't know, do I? In the end he just couldn't tell them. He couldn't tell the police it was me.'

Police, Beth thought. What were they doing out there?

155

Why wasn't anything happening? Why weren't they helping her?

The police had forced everyone to move. Cordoned off the road. Evacuated all the houses. They'd wanted Debra to go home too. Home! As if she could. So they'd compromised. And now all Debra could do was watch from the house diagonally opposite Miriam's. Watch as more police officers arrived. Armed marksmen, psychologists, counsellors. Covering every possibility. And someone else too. Someone else was on their way. But would he get there in time? Would it help anyway?

A lady officer had held Debra's hand. Had assured her that Beth was safe. For the time being. Eddie wouldn't give up the only advantage he had. But to believe that, you had to believe that Eddie was sane, rational. And he couldn't be.

Phones were ringing, people were talking but Debra ignored them all, her eyes fixed on the house over the road, where two plain clothes officers were approaching the door.

'Mr Wilcox?'

Beth heard the voice, as Eddie pushed her towards the door, one arm held tight round her throat, the other pressing the knife against her neck.

What am I going to do? Walk out, that's what. They won't touch me. Not while I've got her. But what then? Where do I go? I can't get out of the country. Maybe I could just lie low for a while. If I can get to my car. Drive off. With the girl. That would do. For a start.

'Stand back,' Eddie shouted. 'All of you. Get away from the door.'

The tread of footsteps retreating. Shout of confirmation that the path was clear.

'Open it,' Eddie told Beth.

Her hands shook, fumbled with the catch.

'Open it!' he snarled.

Beth forced her fingers to grip and twist, pulling the door.

'Wide, open it wide,' said Eddie, stepping back, dragging her with him. 'I want them to see us before we make our move.'

They stood in the doorway, staring at the police in the garden, by the gate, out on the road. Dozens of them. Somehow more than Beth had expected. More than Eddie had expected, too. She could sense his panic, his tension. The knife pressed into her neck, nicking the skin before retracting. Beth started to sob. Urine trickled down her leg.

'Shut up!' Eddie snapped, pushing her forward, her limbs limp in his arms.

'Let the girl go,' a calm, male voice said, somewhere to Beth's left. 'Let the girl go, Mr Wilcox.'

Yeah, as if!

'Move back. All of you. No forward. In front of me. Where I can see you. Do what I say and she'll be just fine,' Eddie said, edging Beth slowly onwards.

'All right Beth, all right,' a strange voice reassured her. 'You're doing great. Just do as he says for the time being. He won't hurt you, will you, Mr Wilcox? You don't really want anybody to get hurt, do you? You didn't want to hurt Debra, did you?'

No, don't start! Don't start winding me up. I'm not listening. I'm not listening.

'You just want people to understand how you feel, don't you, Eddie?'

Eddie now, is it? Trying to make friends, are you? Trying to make me drop my guard! Well, it won't work. I'm not going to answer you. I'm just going to keep walking towards the gate.

'Open the gate! Someone open the bloody gate! Leave it open. Stand back.'

'All right, Eddie,' the voice said. 'You can come out. If you want to. But I'd like you to let the girl go.'

Beth allowed her eyes to move in the direction of the voice. Saw the man, standing alone as everyone else drew back. Casually dressed. Benign expression fixed on his face. Psychologist? Therapist? The voice of reason.

'Let the girl go, Eddie,' the man urged again. 'Then we can talk.'

No talking. No more bloody talking. Where's my car? Where did I leave it? Did I even bring it? I don't know. I can't remember. I can't see it. Not with all these cop cars all over the place. What's happening? Over the road? Another car drawing up. How am I supposed to do anything? With all these bloody cops around? And that idiot talking to me all the time. They can't do this to me. This is my game. I make the rules.

158

'I want them moved! I want all these cars out of the way. Now!'

'Fine. OK, Eddie,' the man said, glancing across the street. 'We'll move everyone, I promise. But there's someone who wants to talk to you, first.'

I'm not talking. Not to anyone. Don't they understand that? I don't care who they're bringing . . . oh shit! Not him. Not him. You can't do this. You can't do this to me!'

'Debra, no!' her dad shouted as she pulled away and rushed downstairs.

She didn't stop. Couldn't stop. Not after what she'd seen. As Gordon Wilcox had walked towards his son, Eddie had panicked. He'd yelled something and pushed Beth forward so hard, that she'd fallen, face down, on the street as Eddie ran off.

'Let me go, let me go,' Debra screamed, as someone grabbed her at the bottom of the stairs, by the open door.

'It's all right,' said the police officer. 'They've got him. He didn't get far.'

'Beth,' Debra shouted. 'I want to see Beth.'

Debra was aware of the policeman relaxing his grip, passing her into the arms of her dad who'd followed her downstairs.

'You can,' the policeman said. 'In a moment. Once they've got Eddie Wilcox away. Your friend's going to be fine, love. I promise. She's going to be OK.'

'How do you know?' Debra snapped, trying to pull away from her dad again, straining to see what was

159

happening outside. 'How do you know what it's like? How she feels?'

'Debra,' said her dad. 'Debra, please.'

Another officer appeared in the doorway.

'Beth's in the ambulance,' he said. 'Her mother's with her but she's asking for you.'

Debra stumbled outside, clutching onto her dad's arm. As she reached the gate, a man was being ushered into a police car. Not Eddie, but his father, Gordon. He turned, looked at Debra, his face grey and strained.

'You're Debra, aren't you?' he said. 'Debra Cardew?'

She nodded.

'I'm sorry,' he said, with tears in his eyes. 'I'm so sorry.'

Chapter 15

Debra looked at her watch.

'Packing up time,' she said, pushing her folder to one side. 'Do you want a drink?'

Beth nodded but continued tapping away on her laptop on the kitchen table.

'I reckon we're doing all right on our own, you know,' Beth said. 'I don't think we need to go back to school!'

'Maybe you don't,' said Debra, smiling. 'But I need all the help I can get. And besides, I sort of miss people, don't you?'

Beth stopped typing and turned to face her.

'Monday then?' she said. 'We'll go back on Monday. Like we said. If you think I'm fit to be seen.'

Debra laughed.

'Sorry,' she said. 'It's not funny. But that plaster on your nose looks ridiculous!'

'It'll be gone by Monday,' said Beth, taking a mirror from her bag. 'And most of the bruises have faded.'

'Is that all that's stopping you going back, then?' asked Debra. 'Vanity?'

Debra knew the answer to the question. Knew it had nothing to do with vanity and, in fact, had precious little to do with Beth at all.

'Definitely!' said Beth. 'There's a couple of new lads in sixth form. I saw 'em on induction day. One of them's dead fit. Don't want to frighten him off, do I?'

161

Debra smiled as she poured the coffee. It was Friday today. Just nine days since Beth's ordeal and exactly a week since Beth had come out of hospital. Yet, apart from the obvious physical injuries, from when Beth was hurled onto the pavement, it would be difficult to tell that anything had happened to her at all. She'd been so brave! Beth, Debra knew, could have faced going back to school at the start of the week, bruises or no bruises but she'd chosen to work at their house. Claiming, of course, that she needed time.

'But what about you?' Beth was asking. 'Are you sure you're up to it?'

There it was. The real reason that Beth had taken time off school. To help her!

'Yes,' said Debra, surprised by her own conviction. 'Yes, I am.'

They'd talked about things, of course. Compared their experiences. Looked for answers. What had made Eddie so warped, so crazy? Why had his dad protected him? Why hadn't Miriam's mum spoken out about her suspicions? There weren't really any answers, certainly not easy ones. But talking to Beth had been better than talking to a counsellor. Beth had been so brave and determined, Debra felt almost compelled to be positive.

'Who's that?' said Beth, as they heard the front door opening.

'Maybe Lori,' said Debra. 'She's been to make some sort of peace with Stefan before she goes back to Uni. I didn't think it was a good idea but you know Lori!

162

She feels sorry for him. The way everyone suspected him at first.'

'Yeah,' said Beth, blushing slightly as, not Lori, but Mrs Cardew came in.

'Mum!' said Debra. 'You're back early!'

She paused, her mother's black suit jolting her memory. Mum had been to a funeral. Alice Hall's funeral.

'It finished at three,' said Mrs Cardew, putting her handbag on the table. 'And, to be honest, I didn't feel like going back into work. I'm not sure I should have gone to the funeral at all. I mean I barely knew the woman but . . .'

Debra put her arms round her, gave her a hug. She hadn't known Mrs Hall either but she'd been shocked when she learnt of the heart attack. Natural causes, the doctors had said, though possibly hastened by the drugs overdose, the stress.

'I'm sorry,' said Mrs Cardew, taking the tissue Beth had passed her.

'It's OK,' Beth said, as her mobile started to bleep.

Debra handed out drinks, then sat silently watching her mum sipping coffee and Beth attending to her text message. There'd been so many messages to both of them over the past week, it was hard to keep track. Not to mention all the letters, phone calls, flowers and cards. Including dozens of calls from Simon, which had cheered her up, a particularly sugary card from Amy & Marc, which had bothered Debra not at all and a short e-mail from Tim Simmonds, which had made her cry. It was upbeat, wishing her well, thanking her for believing in him, with no trace of anger that she'd blurted out his secret. No mention of the court case hanging over him. No hint of self pity.

'It's Miriam,' Beth said. 'On one of her guilt trips again. Silly girl!'

Debra noticed Beth smile faintly, as she spoke. Her words weren't meant unkindly. And they'd both done their best to reassure Miriam over the past week. But it was almost impossible. Miriam, her parents, her uncle, all felt responsible. All felt they should have seen the signs. Should have known how unstable, how dangerous Eddie was becoming.

So many lives messed up, Debra thought. But no. She wouldn't let herself think like that.

'He's not going to ruin everything,' Beth had said, more than once. 'We're not going to let him. Are we, Debs?'

It's stupid. They're making such a big deal of everything. My solicitor says I might be looking at twenty years unless I make out like I'm mentally ill or something. So fat lot of use he is! And Dad. Dad's really doing my head in. But then again he always does. Bleating on about how he's going to stand by me. I suppose by that, he means he'll come visiting every week. Moralizing. Making me feel guilty, as usual. Staring at me with watery eyes, accusing me of letting him down. Or, even worse, accusing himself of letting me down. Of never having had time for me. Always being busy with work and his bloody council. Too keen on keeping up appearances. Not noticing what was festering underneath.

It was Dad who got it all out of me, in the end though. Where I'd kept Debra. I wasn't going to tell the cops. I was going to let them work for their money. Find out for themselves. But Dad sort of guessed anyway. Well he would, wouldn't he? He knew about the properties waiting for development. I'd bought them. I'd done the deals but it was Dad's money. Cash transactions on two of them so they weren't even on the books! That's why I was fairly sure no one would come looking. And they hadn't! I nearly got away with it, didn't I?

Anyway, once Dad had guessed, it was just a case of telling him which one. It was the end terrace, as it happened. Belonged to some old bloke who'd died. The curtains and half the furniture were still in there. So it was ideal. Especially with the alley and massive wall at the back. Made it easy to get in and out of without anybody noticing.

They said it might help my case if I told them everything. Which just shows what a bunch of liars they are. I even told them where I'd hidden the photographs and digital camera. But nothing's going to help, is it? 'Cos they've all got it in for me. I could see it in their eyes. Those cops who interviewed me. They don't like people who mess with kids, do they?

'Have you any idea,' one of them said, 'what both those girls went through?'

'What about me?' I wanted to say. 'Do you think I'm enjoying any of this?'

But I didn't. I just hung my head. Looked contrite. Remorseful. Practising for the trial. Juries like remorse, don't they? Wonder how they feel about regret? I could do regret easy enough. I mean, who in their right mind wouldn't regret being in this sort of mess? But then, I'm not supposed to be in my right mind, am I?

Dad says she insisted on going to look at the house. Debra. She wanted to see where she'd been kept. Insisted on looking at the photographs too. Part of the healing process, Dad said. That's what I mean about fuss. Making everything out to be worse than it is. Like I keep telling them, those photos weren't exactly graphic, were they? And I didn't hurt either of those girls, did I? Not really.

'Come on then, Debs,' Beth said, as they got out of the car. 'This is it!'

She felt a bit of a fraud, grabbing Debra's arm, dragging her through the gates, as though she felt normal, confident, just like before. She might look confident but it was largely illusion. Make–believe. To convince herself, as much as anyone.

She hadn't told Debs about the nightmares. The ones she had every single night. She hadn't told anybody and she wasn't going to. They'd fade in time. She was sure. And until then, she'd keep pretending. It was, she'd decided, the only way.

'Hey!' a voice shouted, as Tonya and Safira rushed up to them. 'It's nearly nine o'clock. We thought you weren't going to turn up!'

'Yeah well,' said Debra, trying to disguise the massive effort it had taken. 'We thought we'd sort of sneak in quietly, without any fuss.'

Tonya and Safira looked at each other, a bit uneasily, as

all four of them stood, for a moment, by the gate, where they'd posed for that photograph, reminding Debra of some news she wanted to tell Beth.

'The police have dropped the charges against Tim,' she said. 'About Evie's death. They say there wasn't enough evidence.'

'So what'll happen now?' Beth asked, as they walked towards school. 'Will he go back to work?'

'He's going to do a couple of days a week, at first,' said Debra. 'Until he gets sorted. He's on tablets for the depression and he's finally agreed to see a counsellor. Recognizing the problem's half the battle, apparently. Hey, where are we going?'

They'd gone through the foyer, past the hall and Debra had tried to turn right, towards the classrooms but Tonya and Safira had steered them left towards the sixth form common room.

'We haven't got time,' Debra said, feeling the sudden clamminess of her hands, the sweat breaking out on her forehead. 'Besides I'd rather go straight to lessons. Just settle back quietly.'

'Whoops,' said Tonya, as Safira pushed open the door. 'Sorry, Debs.'

The cheer hit them seconds before Debra's eyes took in the packed common room, the multi-coloured balloons, the streamers. She glanced at Beth, wondering whether to bolt, go home again but it was too late. Simon had rushed up to her, grabbed her hand, led her inside.

'I told them you probably wouldn't want all this,' he whispered. 'But a few people got a bit carried away.'

'No it's OK,' said Debra, gaining confidence from Simon's reassuring grip and taking her lead from Beth, who was doing a silly twirl in the middle of the room.

Debra felt dozens of eyes watching her, waiting for a response. She wanted to say something, do something, but her chest had tightened, her head was spinning. It was all too much.

'We just wanted,' Simon began. 'To say... well you know...'

He paused, looking at Debra, then looking up, making sure her eyes followed.

She saw the massive banner stretching the whole length of the common room. It was difficult to read, at first, the huge letters were fuzzy, unfocused. She took a couple of deep breaths, as Beth came over to her. Standing between Beth and Simon, Debra felt her muscles starting to relax, her head steadily clearing and her eyes beginning to function again. Beth's words came back to her... 'He's not going to ruin everything. We're not going to let him. Are we, Debs?' Beth was right. It wouldn't, necessarily, be easy for either of them but they'd made a start. A good start.

'Thanks,' Debra managed to say, smiling as the letters finally came into focus and she read the two, simple words on the banner.

'Welcome Back'